MW00744911

Johnny Angel

Tom Tytar

Johnny Angel

AUTHOR'S NOTE: The individual characters who appear in this book are wholly
fictional. No character bears any resemblance to any person, alive or dead, whom I've
ever known. And any apparent resemblance of a character to any person alive or dead
is entirely coincidental.

Print ISBN: 978-1-09832-352-3

eBook ISBN: 978-1-09832-353-0

Cover illustration by Dixie Olin

ONE

"Guy goes to the doctor because he's not feeling well. So, the doctor gives him a bunch of tests and tells him to come back in a couple of days. The dude comes back the next week and he's feeling worse. The doctor tells him his tests are back and he's got some good news and some bad news. The guy thinks about that for a minute then asks the doctor for the bad news first. The doctor tells him he's got two weeks to live. The guy starts to cry. He can't believe it. He's only thirty years old. Been in perfect health. So, he asks the doctor if that's the bad news, what is the good news? The doctor said, 'You know my good-looking receptionist in the lobby with the 34 double D's? Well I'm screwing her.'"

The comedian telling this lame old joke got the biggest laugh of his stale routine. His name was Slats, and he's been laying a bomb on the stage of Detroit's Empress Burlesque for the last ten minutes. Slats wore a rumpled gray suit with big lapels and looked to be pushing eighty. His eyes were glassy and bloodshot and his speech was slurred like a skid row drunk. Courtesy of too many swigs from a bottle of Jack Daniels he kept backstage. The laughs came from a crowd of white college and high school aged boys decked out in their off-white Levi's, penny loafers, Kingston Trio button down shirts, and crew cut hair. They weren't here for the jokes. They wanted to see some skin.

It was the Saturday before Christmas, 1962, and watching over this circus from the back of the theater was Detroit Vice cop John Angelo. Forty years old, with sandy blonde hair courtesy of an Irish mom. He wore a slim fitting black suit, white shirt with a gold pin through the collar, and a skinny yellow tie.

City ordinance said strippers can take their tops off, can even show their nipples, but exposing anything too far below the belly button got a fine and a couple of nights in lock up. Angelo's been watching a succession of young girls up on stage peeling off baby doll pajamas and Fredericks of Hollywood lingerie, strutting their stuff to top ten tunes. It was nothing like the old days, when the likes of Tempest Storm, Blaze Starr, Betty Paige, and the goddess of Burlesque, Gypsy Rose Lee, made it an art form. The grace, elaborate costumes, the tease; all but forgotten. A memory stored on fading 16-millimeter color film. Now it was twist again like we did last summer, then throw in a few steps of the locomotion.

Most of the dancers were young and pretty good looking. Just out of high school, or maybe in their early twenties. They could have been somebody's girlfriend or wife. Girls serving burgers at the Big Boy or whipping up ice cream sundaes at Saunders, instead of prancing around naked in a gaudy old burlesque joint. If Angelo did his job, they all would have been busted for indecent exposure. But he's got a crisp new twenty that the bouncer, Big Bill, slipped him when he took his normal lookout post, so the hell with the City Ordinance. For a Vice cop on the take, Angelo took pretty small.

As bouncers go, Big Bill wasn't that big. He stood about five feet six thanks to lifts in his shoes with a hunch-shouldered frame. What were big were the arms. Biceps the size of cantaloupes, and a chest almost busting out of his tight white t-shirt. Bill pumped iron with a set of old Joe Weider barbells he kept in the theater's basement. He slept there too, on a cot in one of the girl's dressing rooms. During the day he washed dishes at the White Tower around the corner for a buck-twenty an hour plus meals. Bill was one happy camper. Three squares a day and all those naked young women to ogle at night.

Big Bill chewed on a wad of Redman tobacco and used a rusty bucket as a spittoon, kept out of sight in the back of the theater. And when he spoke Angelo could see the hard, yellowed edges of his teeth.

"You just missed her, John."

"Just missed who?"

"New girl. Calls herself Honeypie. Never been on stage before. She did okay. Little nervous at first, but really seemed to get into it. I talked to her before we opened tonight. Think she took a shine to me. Told me she used to be a Fuller Brush salesgirl. Door to door. Damn! Can you imagine a broad like her knocking on your front door? I'm thinking about seeing if she wants to get a drink after the show."

Angelo let that ride. The girls let Big Bill look but never got palsey-walsey with him.

"How many ID's did you check tonight?"

"Chased a bunch of thirteen-year old boys out of here last night. Asked them what school they went to. They all told me Ensley Junior High." And with that Big Bill spit in the bucket, then went and stood on the other side of the theater. The Empress was short and narrow. You could probably fit a dozen of them into the main floor of the Fox movie theater a couple of blocks up Woodward Avenue.

It was close to midnight, the last of two shows, with the final act coming on stage now. Her name was Lillian Rose, barked the announcer, which was her stage name. Her birth name Rose Horschak. In her mid-thirties, with Technicolor red hair and skin white as a cup of heavy cream, she was a good ten years older than the other dancers. She went by the nickname of Lil' Red. Lil' Red wore one of those Japanese silk robes decorated with flowers that hid everything down to her ankles. Her sequined silver stiletto heels glittered under the hot stage lights as she danced seductively to the first tune, a twangy Duane Eddy guitar instrumental.

The crowd quiet, patient, waited for that kimono to hit the floor. The next song was all tease; *A Summer Place* by Percy Faith. She showed some leg, then, a peek at a bare shoulder. Chants from the young boys of 'take it off!' But she didn't. The crowd booed when the song ended.

The last song was a new one, *Johnny Angel*. Just broke into Billboard's Top Ten. And that's when Angelo got the inkling that the song was directed at him. Some of the strippers at the National Burlesque further up Woodward Avenue started calling him Johnny Angel after one of the taxi-dance girls at the Woodland Ballroom pinned that on him.

About a minute into the song Lil' Red elegantly slipped out of that kimono and there she was in all her nakedness. Not even a G-sting. Just a show-biz smile and gleaming white teeth. The boys were now gleefully coming out of their seats. To raucous hoots and hollers, she gracefully slow danced across the stage, shaking this and that. When the song ended Lil' Red took a graceful bow and gave Angelo a military salute as the house came down with thunderous applause, and for John Angelo, the inkling was gone, it was all about him.

Later, Lil' Red sat at the makeup table in her shabby dressing room in the basement of the theater. The Empress was built around 1908 and was first used as a movie theater, then vaudeville, and for the past twenty years burlesque. The Empress was no plushy club and it showed its age. There was no ceiling in the basement, just all the exposed plumbing and heating pipes wrapped in white asbestos. As the headliner, Lil' Red had her own dressing room and private bath, which she considered the basis of civilization.

The dressing room door eased open, Angelo slid into the room, leaned up against the dirty, faded yellow wall, in the sight line of Lil' Red looking in her mirror.

She said, "How'd you like my act and the new song?"

In one smooth continuous motion, Angelo flipped a Chesterfield out of the pack, puts it between his lips, snapped open a Zippo, the flame glowing in the muted light.

"Now that was a catchy tune, but you're gonna have to tell Big Bill it'll take another ten spot or you'll have to keep your bottoms on till the end of the song."

"You're funny. Maybe you can replace Slats. He asked me to bake him a birthday cake. He's turning seventy next week. Keeps talking about retiring."

"Angelo said, I guess you've been talking to the girls up at the National?"

Lil' Red smeared a small dab of Ponds cold cream over her cheeks, fingers heavy with rings, as the makeup lights danced on her red hair.

"No. I've been talking to Sophia Martino up at the Woodland Ballroom. We were comparing notes. She said she has one of your apartment keys. Getting kind of chummy, huh?"

Angelo was caught flat footed for a moment. They'd both been putting out for him. It wasn't a secret. The girls knew the situation, but Sophia's key threw a monkey wrench into the works and he wasn't going to let Lil' Red's comment drift with the tide.

Angelo said, "Hey, I didn't change the lock."

She looked at Angelo with large moist eyes.

"Sophia's fifty-five, wants to retire, but thirty years of two-bits a dance and five-dollar hand jobs won't do the trick. You feeling sorry for her, or are you really into older spaghetti-bending dames?"

Angelo mulled that over a couple seconds, kept that Chesterfield hanging on his lower lip, ready to crack wise.

"What, you want me to ask you to go steady?"

And with that, Lil' Red wiped the cold cream from her face, swiveled around on the stool, got up, then walked slow and seductive to him.

She took the Chesterfield from his lips, inhaled a deep drag, and blew a perfect smoke ring into his face.

"I'm waiting for a guy on a white horse to ride down the aisle one night, carry me out of this shit hole and buy me a little sweetness and light."

She untied her silk kimono, pulled him in tight to her nakedness. Made him feel everything she had. Everything those kids in rows A through Z could only look at and fantasize about. Lil' Red gave him a sloppy wet kiss.

"But… Johnny Angel, I guess this is as good as it's going to get."

TWO

It was half-past midnight. Traffic was light on Woodward Avenue. Angelo headed north in a black, unmarked 1960 Ford Galaxy he checked out at Police Headquarters over at 1300 Beaubien. With a straight six cylinder and three on the tree, it was a real dog, but got him to where he needed to go on his regular shift of six until two in the morning. Where he needed to go right now was the Woodland Ballroom for a conversation with Sophie Martino.

Angelo hated conflict, especially in his personal life, and didn't want the nonsense of Lil' Red and Sophia cat-fighting it out over his attention. He was a vice cop on the take, pocketing some extra cash on the side for looking the other way. Hell, it's what made the payments on that cream color 58 Chevy Bel Air with the shiny red vinyl interior. He bought it new at Trumbull Chevrolet on Michigan Avenue, right across the street from Tiger Stadium. With only one payment left, his life was pretty smooth for a vice cop. Go along to get along. Take-it-and-get greed. Nothing long term. He wasn't about to let a stripper and taxi dancer disrupt the normal flow of things in his world.

Yeah, he was sleeping with both of them, but Sophia was more of a mercy situation. She'd make some home cooked Italian meal for him, then come on to him hot and heavy, so it was hard to say no.

The Woodland Ballroom was on the second floor of a building on the west side of Woodward, a couple of blocks north of the Fox Theater. The main floor was vacant and the upstairs had been operating as a taxi-dance emporium since the 1930's so it was pretty shabby.

For a Saturday night, business was a little slack. A team of women plied a hodge-podge of male customers with cute come-ons, and false compliments, all packaged in rat-teased hair, tight fitting girdles, push up bras, and patent leather high heels.

Most of the women were looking for extra cash, turn-ing tricks after hours at one of the hot sheet motels further up Woodward near Eight-mile Road. Sophia was the oldest dancer at the club. Most of the girls were in their thirties and forties. For a hooker, working here was better than standing on a corner, or getting tossed out of the bar at the Embassy Hotel on a cold December night. In the dim light, one of the games girls played was to dance a john into a corner, let him cop a feel if he slipped a few bucks down her cleavage. Management didn't care, long as they get their cut.

Angelo made his way across the moody dimness of the dance floor looking for Sophia. Maybe cut in if he had to. But she was nowhere to be found. The scratchy old Hi-Fi belted out an old Glenn Miller tune. Back in the day they actually had a full piece band. Angelo walked over to the ticket window run by a woman named Maude, one of the owners. Maude was a hard-faced woman in her sixties with foxy little eyes, not bad looking, but packing on a few pounds. Bragged how she used to dance at the Stone Burlesque in her younger days. She saw Angelo approach.

"No sixteen-year-old virgins in here, Angelo, you know I run a tight ship."

"I'm looking for Sophia, she working tonight?"

"You missed her, punched out at midnight."

"She leave with anybody?"

"Not with one of the regulars. Some young colored dude with black leather pants. Can you believe that? Leather pants almost as tight as a pair of nylons; paid me ten bucks and danced her right off the floor."

"She say anything, where she was going?"

"Had a big wad of bills he rolled that ten spot off. Colored guy can afford leather pants, gotta be a high-roller. I'd check the Embassy.

Angelo checked the bar at the Embassy Hotel, and before that a couple of the motels near Eight-Mile. Nada. He headed home now in his Bel-Air sedan after clocking out. A few snowflakes speckled the windshield as he made his way east on Jefferson to his garden apartment in an old brownstone about a block from the Belle Isle Bridge.

His apartment door was unlocked. He thought about slipping out the hide-away .38 special he kept strapped to his leg just above the ankle. On second thought, after what went down tonight at the Empress, it must be Lil' Red. He pushed the door open, and flicked on the light switch. The living room was trashed. The brand-new sofa he just bought at Hudson's was slit open and all the stuffing ripped out. The kitchenette turned upside down. Plates and glasses in jagged pieces littered the floor.

He slid the .38 from his pant leg and moved to the bedroom. It looked like a small tornado hit the place. His clothes and belongings were scattered about. But what caught his eye was the Murphy bed pulled down from the wall. Lil' Red and Sophia Martino lay on the bed. Both of them were naked, beaten, and all bloodied up with gunshots in the forehead and chest.

THREE

The interrogation room at Detroit Police Headquarters needed redecorating. Any color but dirty gray would spruce the place up a bit, but just how serene and comfortable would you want to make it? Sweating a confession out of a suspect seemed more in line with harsh light diffused by cigarette smoke, and an overall bad vibe.

That vibe was getting under Angelo's skin now that he was the one getting grilled. Two homicide detectives, Stan Kowalski and Eddie Proul fired questions at him left and right. Kowalski and Proul had been on the force since 1935. They both started out as beat cops and eventually worked their way up to homicide. Their reputations preceded them. They were racist thugs with nothing upstairs but solid knuckle who terrorized the poor black neighborhood of Paradise Valley, east of Woodward Avenue. During the race riots of 1943 that began on Belle Isle, Kowalski threw a black teenager off the Belle Isle Bridge. That was the rumor that circulated around the department. True or not, Kowalski wore it like a badge of honor.

The two self-aggrandizing hot shots worked like prize fighters trying to land verbal punches, softening Angelo up, then going for a knockout. In this case, to make him spill his guts, copping to the murders of Sophia and Lil' Red. They were batting zero. Proul leaned into Angelo.

"Tell us now, what's it like screwing two floozies at the same time?"

Kowalski said, "Maybe like that eight-millimeter stag film at Holliman's retirement party last month. You screw the one broad, while the other one-."

"The other one what?"

That brought a laugh from Proul and Kowalski, thinking they're going to piss him off, break him, get him to confess. The look on Angelo's face said it wasn't working.

"Gee, I'm sorry I missed Holliman's party and that hot smoker. So, did you all sit around and have a circle jerk?"

Proul parked one cheek of his fat ass on the table where Angelo sat and with a little-rascal like grin on his puffy face, lit up a Lucky Strike with the flick of a kitchen match, and blew a plume of smoke in Angelo's face.

"Okay wise guy, cut the shit. Why the fuck did you kill both bitches?"

Angelo was stomaching their bullshit, staying cool.

"Let me lay it out for you. You guys are lazy. You wanna wrap this up quick, get home in time for Sunday Mass with the wife and kids. So, let's suppose I'd sign something says I did it. I get in front of the prosecutor. He tells me I'm looking at life without parole, maybe take a plea for manslaughter. Get maybe ten to fifteen. But I've got something else. Bank accounts in Windsor under phony names. I got one. Both of you dopes each got one. Shit, half the department is on the take. See what I'm saying? I ain't going down alone. So, unless you got any little piddling things you wanna hang on me, I'm done."

The sun was just coming up over the horizon on this December Sunday morning reflecting a half-light shadow on the neon lit sign of the Red Arrow Motel on Woodward Ave, a block south of Seven Mile Road.

Angelo parked his car, checked in at the front desk, and picked up a key to room eighteen. It would be a while before he could get back into his apartment, even to get a change of clothes. Maybe Monday. Maybe Tuesday. All depended on how quick police investigators worked their magic. Anything found, he'd want to know.

He wasn't homicide anymore, just a dumb vice cop, but he was going to work this case come hell or high water. Now, he just wanted to sleep. As he flopped himself down on that double bed, all he could think about was sleep. A hundred hours might do the trick, he told himself.

Angelo tossed and turned for a couple of hours. No level of dead tiredness could keep his mind from churning. He threw the blanket back on the bed, sat up, took a look at the noisy electric clock bolted to the end table. It read seven-thirty a.m.

He turned on the seventeen-inch TV, also bolted down. Sonny Elliot, the local weatherman was giving his sing-song, chipper forecast for the day. Cold and windy with a high of thirty and a chance of snow showers.

Angelo lit a cigarette, sat there a moment and watched Sonny the weatherman performing his daily comedy bit. He even managed a little grin at one of Sonny's jokes.

Angelo had to move fast, get on this case before Kowalski and Proul started stumbling their way through it on Monday morning, mucking things up. Hot shower, then a cup of coffee at the White Tower next door, sounded like a good start.

Sonny the weatherman was dead on. Big wet snow flakes melted on the windshield as Angelo parked his car on a side street just off Jefferson, a couple of blocks from his apartment. He watched two young guys in a rowing scull on the Detroit River slip under the Belle Isle Bridge.

He had to turn in his apartment key back at headquarters. If he was caught rummaging around his apartment before police investigators, it would look like he was destroying evidence, or covering up. That's why he parked on Jefferson.

He had to be stealthy. A key hidden behind a loose brick got him into his apartment.

Everything was just as he left it, except Lil' Red and Sophia had been shipped to metal slabs at Wayne County Morgue. Wanting to search the place for any kind of clue, without disturbing the crime scene, was going to be a real kick in the head.

He started to look for anything and everything that might be out of the ordinary.

This was the juice, the way he figured it. Lil' Red skipped on over here after he left her at the Empress, got naked again, and slipped under the covers, waiting for him after his shift ended at two.

Sophia left the Woodland Ballroom with the black guy sporting the tight leather pants. They came here because the dude was looking for something that he wanted bad enough to trash the place, and ice the two of them. Did he find it? Was Lil' Red involved in the something he wanted so bad, or was she just in the wrong place at the wrong time? Those were just two of the sixty-four thousand-dollar questions.

After about a half hour of coming up empty, Angelo parked himself on an ottoman a couple of feet in front of the TV. The morning sun was getting higher now, and a stream of gold light bounced off the screen of the old Sylvania. As he sat there, he couldn't help but think about Lil' Red and Sophia. Couple of crazy dames no doubt, both with some off-key neurotic charm, but underneath, looking for something better, that neither of them was ever going to find. He remembered how Lil' Red used to talk about going to Hollywood, maybe try some modeling, or hang around outside the movie studios, get discovered.

Sophia, in all her fifty-five years had never been south of Toledo, north of Flint, or west of Ann Arbor. She just watched TV. Her favorite show was a Sunday show on Channel 4. A local travelogue hosted by George Perot.

She'd tell Angelo how the guy was so old he'd fall asleep while the guest was narrating his trip to France, or wherever the fuck it was. That's how Sophia escaped. She'd laugh and tell Angelo how when she quit work, she'd travel the world and make home movies, come back to Detroit, go on George Perot's show and watch the old fart fall asleep in his big leather chair.

FOUR

Nat Hollywood, not his real last name, which was Cain, rolled out of bed this December Sunday morning, slipped his Rolex Submariner watch onto his wrist and checked the time. It was eleven-thirty.

He made his way into the kitchen, popped open the Frigidaire, and chugged the remaining contents of a bottle of Twin Pines milk the milkman left outside his front door Friday morning. Nat's apartment wasn't big, but it sure was decorated nice.

Comfy plush red sofa, twenty-five-inch color TV with a retail price of one grand he lifted off the back of an Adray Appliance delivery truck one hot summer night. His only regret was not boosting a window air conditioner that night. About the only thing on TV in color was *Bonanza* on Sunday night. Nat hated Westerns, but took pride in owning a color TV while watching all those dopey sitcoms in black and white.

Nat strolled over to the living room front window. He stood there in his red and white striped pajamas and watched light traffic on West Grand Boulevard. Snowflakes collected and wet the windshield of his 1956 Cadillac Fleetwood parked on the street. Cadillac's top of the line. A one owner he hot-wired from the driveway of a rich old white widow who lived in Indian Village. He paid close to a grand for a new paint job, and new serial numbers courtesy of a chop shop on the east side.

Nat set the empty milk bottle on the kitchen counter then headed back to the bedroom and opened the closet door. A line of shiny sharkskin suits, mostly black, a few blue, lined the closet on neatly spaced hangers. All compliments of a late-night break-in at the Hudson's warehouse.

He selected a black suit, unfolded a newly laundered red silk shirt, and got dressed. He topped it off with a skinny black tie then slipped on some over the calf black socks and pointy toe black leather Florsheim's.

Back in the living room, looking pretty swank, Nat stood in front of a MacIntosh stereo system that he boosted from a house out in Bloomfield Hills a couple of months ago. The whole system cost around six hundred bucks new. Not only did the system put out great sound, but it lit up the room like fireworks when you put the lights out. All those tubes glowed and sparkled.

He sorted through a stack of records, selected one, placed it on the turntable, set the needle onto the first groove, then assumed a performing stance in front of the big speakers. The pure sound of Smokey Robinson filled the room. Dressed like he was going to a Sunday service, Nat sang along as backup on the song *Shop Around*. His voice was pretty damn smooth. Like a high baritone in a choir, but it wasn't the Baptist Church next door he was practicing for.

FIVE

John Angelo sat behind the wheel of his '58 Bel Air parked on a side street two blocks north of Warren Avenue on Detroit's west side. He was in front of Sophia's house. It was a small, white clapboard story-and-a-half. He'd been here only once before, so it was good that he remembered the house number.

All the houses on the street were white story-and-a-half, built just after the war on the cheap to qualify for VA loans. The one time he'd been there was for dinner. The best damn pasta primavera he'd ever tasted, with home-baked garlic bread and a Caesar salad. The wine was a cheap Dago red, but it washed things down pretty well with just enough of a buzz.

When Sophia pulled him in to the downstairs bedroom for some extracurricular messing around, he didn't mind so much. The fifty-five years showed some on her face and body and smoking four packs of Lucky Strikes a day made her a little weak in the lungs, but she had all the right moves, wasn't anything she wasn't into and at fifteen years his senior taught him things he could never even have fantasized about in high school.

That was the first time they got it on. She gave him a house key, but he never used it. Couple of times she came over to his place to cook him dinner, they'd jump in the sack, but he always felt a little bit guilty after. But not as guilty as he felt now, sitting there with her house key in his hand, and her dead body lying in the morgue.

The inside of Sophia's house was what you'd expect from a down on her luck fifty-five-year old taxi-dancer and hooker. In other words, there was nothing special about it. Plain and cheap. A worn sofa was pushed up against a bare wall. Couple of flimsy looking end tables pretended to grace the ends of the sofa. The TV was an old Zenith, one of those early 50's models with a round fourteen-inch screen. The carpet was just another thing on the floor. It was an old, fusty, dirty and bitter room with enough junk lying around to take a month to dust.

Angelo looked around in a haphazard way and found nothing that meant anything, then made his way into the downstairs bedroom. An unmade double bed he remembered as being pretty bouncy was for some reason square in the middle of the room.

There was an old dresser against one wall that someone had stripped of its finish. He remembered that, but what was on top wasn't there before. It was a framed photo of a young man about twenty years old, dressed in an Army uniform. What was striking about it was that the soldier looked like Angelo in his younger days. A dead ringer with the same hair, same shaped face, and dark eyes.

Angelo wore that same uniform back in 1945 as a combat military policeman tracking down rapists, deserters and murderers as Allied forces pushed toward Berlin.

Sophia never talked about any man in her life. What rushed to the front of his mind was the thought that the home cooked Italian fare and sexual favors were about him replacing that guy, whoever he was. Maybe the guy walked out on her, sent her one of those Dear Jane letters, or God forbid, got his ticket punched in WWII.

He didn't want to think about it anymore as he made his way to the upstairs bedroom, a place he'd never been before. Whatever decorating skills Sophia lacked evidenced by the downstairs drab, it was a one-eighty on the second level. The room walls were hot pink in color. The ceiling was painted bright white. Silk sheets on the bed glistened a satiny pearl. And mountains of red pillows, enough to stuff a horse, were propped up against a brass headboard. Some sexy bright red lingerie was slung over the headboard.

On either side of the double bed stood photographic lights mounted on tripods. There was one more tripod. It stood between the two lights. Mounted on it was an expensive French Beaulieu eight-millimeter movie camera. Hmmm, for making one of those travelogue flicks Sophia loved?

SIX

Angelo opened the empty film compartment of the Beaulieu eight-millimeter camera and admired the precision look and feel of it. He was back at the Red Arrow motel on Woodward having stashed the photo lights and tripods in the trunk of his car. He knew that Kowalski and Proul would get around to checking out Sophia's place, and he didn't need them figuring out her little hobby.

He marveled at the way the camera rested in his hand, light but solid, with a turret of three German Leica lenses, close up, wide angle, and normal. If you wanted to film anything of quality on a tiny strip of film, barely a quarter inch wide, then this was the ticket. Miles away from a cheap Kodak wind up.

He checked his watch. It was past one in the afternoon. Many of the Detroit bars would be open now, and he had one in particular he wanted to check out, the Anchor on Michigan Avenue.

The Anchor Bar was a couple of blocks from Tiger Stadium. You could call it a sports bar, but the only thing sporty about it was that players from the Tigers and Lions would sometimes hang out there after games. The Anchor wasn't part of Angelo's beat. The owners ran an up and up joint. A shot and a beer kind of place. They kept it clean, tossed out the drunks, and if you were a hooker looking to score a john, then you'd better look someplace else.

Angelo entered through the rear door. There were a couple of men sitting at the bar watching the Lions play the Cleveland Browns on the black and white TV. An old couple, dressed like they'd just come from church, sat at a table drinking Stroh's beer from the bottle.

The bartender, Fred Nowak, had worked there since the early fifties. He was in his sixties, solid built like a boxer who just broke training. He recognized Angelo.

"Johnny Angel, what brings a Wop all the way to Corktown?" What can I get ya?"

It wasn't the word Wop that got under Angelo's skin, it was the Johnny Angel crack.

"Sophia Martino's been hanging around here, huh? Give me a Canadian Club on the rocks, Fred. Make it a double."

"I didn't mean nothin' by that Johnny Angel crack. Thought you might be okay with it. Got a nice ring to it. Yeah, Sophia's been in but she knows better than to turn tricks outta here."

"When was she here last?"

"Couple of nights ago."

"Anybody with her?"

"All by her lonesome. She ordered her usual, couple bottles of Blatz, and two Wild Turkey chasers."

Angelo took a pull on the Canadian Club.

"Tell me something, Fred. Know anybody peddling high quality stag films on color eight-millimeter?"

That riled Fred up a bit. Got his eyes mad.

"Now look, Angelo, you know the bosses don't allow that shit out of here."

"Yeah, but Fred, you used to be the man with the cam."

"That was ten years ago. And I only worked in black and white. Besides, I got religion now. My old lady made me see the light."

"Good for you, but you must remember somebody."

"Look, black and white you can develop in your kitchen sink. You don't have to be Ansel Adams. Color, if it's Kodachrome, you got to mail to a Kodak lab, so you'd just be askin' the Feds to come down on you like stink on shit. Agfacolor, Ansco, you could do that at home with the right chemicals, but it ain't cheap."

"Thanks for the education, but you still haven't given me a name."

Fred wasn't one to ask for trouble.

"Okay, there's a camera shop out on Van Dyke near Six Mile. Guy named Walt Robbins runs the place. I think he's still there. He used to develop my black and white and make me prints, but I don't think he was set up to do any color."

Angelo downed the last swig of his Canadian Club, and dropped three bucks on the bar.

"Much appreciate that, Fred, and say hi to your old lady for me. Tell her I said she's got a good man."

Angelo drove Michigan Avenue east to Woodward, made a left, and headed back to the Red Arrow motel. Traffic on Woodward was busy for a Sunday afternoon. He passed the closed Empress Burlesque on the corner of Congress. Sunday and Monday would have been Lil' Red's days off.

He thought about checking her apartment over near Palmer Park, but she never gave him a key. She always liked to go to his place when she had the itch, but it wasn't on a regular basis. She just liked surprising him now and then. Turning the lights out and crawling under the covers.

He knew she was giving it up to other guys, and not for free. But it didn't bother him at the time, what bothered him now was the thought that nobody would care about her since she was dead. He knew she had a father somewhere, but nothing else about her life. She didn't talk a lot.

She liked jazz. Miles Davis, Chet Baker. Made him take her to Baker's Keyboard Lounge one night to see The Ahmad Jamal Trio. She sat there in the front row, feet up on the stage, chain smoking Viceroys while downing half a dozen rum and Cokes. It was about the only time he could remember her being content, at peace with the world. Maybe the only time he ever saw her really smile.

He wondered how she got hooked up with Sophia. Did she do nasty things on those satin sheets when Sophia called 'action' and rolled the camera?

He wanted to check out Lil' Red's apartment, but he'd have to break in, and that was off the table. He wasn't going to give Proul and Kowalski any kind of motive served up on a silver platter. Long as he stayed one step ahead of the nimrods, he just might crack this case.

Angelo stopped at a liquor store and bought a bottle of Canadian Club. Back at the Red Arrow he got a bucket of ice from the machine, keyed himself into his room and made himself a drink, then flicked on the TV. Walter Robbins, guy who owned the camera store on Van Dyke had an unlisted home phone number, so he'd have to wait until business hours on Monday morning.

Angelo clicked through the three local channels, settled on Channel 4, the local NBC station, then flopped on the bed. He took a pull on his glass of Canadian Club, and watched the last few seconds of a Colgate toothpaste commercial before George Perot introduced his guest with a travelogue on the wonders of ancient Egypt.

He thought about getting up and changing the channel, but he was too tired to move. Maybe it would put him to sleep. Sure enough, it did. And when he woke up, there was George Perot on TV counting sheep in his big leather chair.

SEVEN

Nat Hollywood stood in the middle of the main dance floor of the Graystone Ballroom gazing up at the beautiful arched ceiling as the music of Martha and the Vandellas boomed in his ears. But it wasn't a recording. It was them in the flesh, up on stage.

The place was rocking with the Motown sound, coined by DJs, and sweeping the country. Sunday night at the Graystone was where Berry Gordy, founder of the Motown record label, had all his singers polish their acts. They worked on new songs, the look he wanted them to present. Many of them were raised in public housing, some school dropouts.

Gordy taught them how to dress, how to talk, how to fit into white society. But he didn't have to teach them how to sing. Mary Wells, Marvin Gaye, Jackie Wilson, the Four Tops, The Supremes, drop a name of any Motown artist, they all worked out at the Graystone on Sunday nights.

The place had its history. Built in the 1920s, every musician from Louis Armstrong to Glenn Miller played the Graystone.

And on this cold December night in 1962 Motown was making a new history.

Nat was grooving to the music, dancing in place in those barely broken in Florsheim's, that black sharkskin suit tight as Saran Wrap on his lean frame. Nat's hair was slicked back. He liked to wear it like Duke Ellington with a little wave in it.

Nat wasn't raised in public housing, and he managed to graduate from high school. He didn't need Berry Gordy to teach him how to dress, how to talk, how to get along with white folks. He'd been doing that since proudly marching across the stage at Mumford High to pick up his diploma. Standing there in the middle of the Graystone, surrounded by hundreds of other well-dressed black music fans, Nat knew that his time would come, he'd be up there on the stage singing lead, or back-up for some new Motown act. All it took was an audition at Motown head-quarters, a few blocks up West Grand Boulevard from his apartment. And Nat was working on that.

EIGHT

The house was huge, even by Grosse Pointe standards. It would give the old Edsel Ford or Dodge Brothers estates a run for their money. Built in the early 40's by steel magnate Charles Turnbull for his retirement home on the shore of Lake St. Clair, it had everything. Indoor pool. Bowling alley.

In his seventies when it was completed, old man Turnbull never got to dog-paddle around in that pool, nor bowl a few lanes in the basement. A massive stroke put him flat on his back in a hospital bed placed in the downstairs library so he could look out the window at the passing iron ore boats and freighters that cruised by day and night.

When he died, his son, Charles II, took over the steel business and the house. Charlie, as he was known, kept the steel mill running until a couple of bad business decisions put him under. Charlie died in that same downstairs library in 1960. But he didn't pass away peacefully watching the boats go by. Blew his head off with a Winchester pump. That was after he put a round in his wife Madge's back, and watched her bleed out on the floor.

Charlie and Madge left the house to their only son Andy, the family fuck up and skirt-chaser, who managed to suck up to his grandfather to the tune of a twenty-five million-dollar trust fund. Andy tapped into that fund on his twenty-fifth birthday and moved into the estate with his older wife Velma.

Since moving in they've lived like debauched royalty. Wild-ass, skinny dipping pool parties and a game Velma invented called strip bowling were common on weekends at the house. Those were the facts, but in the uptight high society circles of the Pointes, they were just rumors flung around by jealous socialites.

A black Ford Galaxy wound its way up the long driveway of the Turnbull estate and one of the doors on the six-car garage opened automatically as the car slid into an empty spot. Homicide cops Kowalski and Proul crawled out of the car and walked by a Mercedes Gull Wing, one of those new Jaguar XKE's, and a 55 T-Bird. Summer cars collecting dust.

A brand new 63 Cadillac covered in Detroit road salt was parked by the interior door, which was opened by Velma Turnbull. Velma was forty years old, with a short page boy black hairdo that framed a cherubic face, a go-to-hell look in her eyes and very plump kissable lips. She was barely dressed in a crimson red silk robe that stopped mid-thigh, revealing a pair of nicely shaped legs. In her hand was a large glass of orange juice as she welcomed Proul and Kowalski into the kitchen.

"Gentlemen, thank you for coming on such short notice. Please have a seat."

Proul and Kowalski parked themselves at the round marble kitchen table. Kowalski spoke first.

"Not a problem, Mrs. Turnbull, what can we do for you?"

Velma sashayed over to a kitchen cabinet drawer with a very noticeable sway of the hips, pulled out a large manila envelope and placed it on the table in front of them.

"I know you are aware that my husband Andy and I have a… rather unconventional lifestyle."

Proul tried to keep his eyes focused where they should be, but wasn't having much luck. He remembered his reaction when he first laid eyes on Mrs. Turnbull. A dame with a platinum chassis. She was dressed to the nines then. Now in that slinky red robe, it was all he could do to put a coherent sentence together. He focused his eyes up to hers.

"To each his own. Not here to judge, Mrs. Turnbull."

"You can call me Velma."

The cops managed a couple of slick smiles. Proul thinking how he'd give up a month's pay just to see the goodies under that robe. Velma opened the envelope and spread four eight by ten black and white photos in front of them. No need to surrender any paycheck because the photos were Velma in the flesh having sex with four young muscular, well-endowed black men.

Proul shot a look at Kowalski. Both of them embarrassed, looking at the explicit photos as Velma stood there calm and collected drinking her orange juice, like she just showed them photos from a trip to Disneyland.

"Let me be up front with both of you. They did not kidnap me. They didn't rape me. Everything in those photos I did of my own choosing. Nobody forced me to do anything."

Kowalski flipped the four photos over.

"Are you trying to shock us, embarrass us, what do you want, Mrs. Turnbull?"

Velma turned the photos right side up, forced them to look. There was a flash of anger in her eyes.

"I want you to find these four boys."

Proul stared at the photos, shuffling them around, trying to be cool.

"You didn't make these dudes wear rubbers?"

Velma stayed calm, playing it tough as an oak board, but these two palookas were starting to grate on her.

"Look. I like sex, especially with younger men. This envelope showed up on my doorstep this morning with a note demanding one hundred thousand dollars or they would send the photos to my husband."

Kowalski tapped his fingers on the table, picked up one of the photos for a closer look.

"Hundred-grand. Nice round figure. Who took the pictures?"

"Andy would kill me if he knew I was fucking colored guys. He'd divorce me. Leave me without a cent. I like this house, that new Jag, and my T-Bird. I've got a closet full of fancy clothes upstairs, some never worn, didn't even open the boxes."

Velma was desperate now. Grinding her teeth.

"You've got to help me!"

Kowalski picked up another photo, glared at it with his glassy little eyes.

"You didn't answer my question. Who took the pictures?"

Velma hemmed and hawed, like she had something to hide. She figured she better come at this from another angle.

"You both know her. You set her up to entertain at my parties. Sophia Martino. She's a taxi-dancer at some club on Woodward."

That got a rise from the two cops.

Proul said, "Sophia Martino. Yeah."

He looked over at Kowalski. Kowalski had a smile on his face of a man whose mind was not smiling.

"You and your husband ever take a tumble with a little red-head named Lilian Rose? Dances at the Empress Burlesque, goes by the name Lil' Red."

Velma was getting the feeling they were trying to flip the switch on her, maybe get her to dime somebody out. Husband Andy and her tumbled a couple of redheads, but that name didn't register.

Velma reached for a bottle of vodka and poured a couple of fingers into her orange juice and took a long sip. She licked her lips and cocked one hip, playing it girly-girl, a real trouser-rouser.

She gave these two cops who looked like they'd been knocked a half-dozen rungs down Darwin's ladder a penetrating look that hit them both like dumdum bullets.

"Andy and I double-teamed a redhead once. But that was at the condo in Tampa Bay. Lil' Red? Name doesn't ring a bell."

Kowalski stared at her a moment, wanting to give her a little heart-to-heart, then blurted out.

"Your photographer Sophia Martino and Lil' Red both got murdered last night."

That knocked the wind out of Velma like a punch to the gut. She took a seat. Her lips trembled as she tried to compose herself.

Kowalski said, "You know anything about that?"

Velma stared at the wall a moment, an absent stare, trying to put her thoughts together.

"No."

Kowalski and Proul shared a look. Was she trying to pull a fast shuffle on them? Maybe they had her in a dead-level moment. They waited for her to break, but Velma wasn't having any of it.

Proul said, "Where is your husband?"

"Andy's in Florida. He'll be back next Sunday."

Kowalski said, "Who are these guys?"

Velma pointed at one of the boys.

"Skinny guy's name is Germaine. He's a busboy at the Belle Isle Boat Club. That's what his name tag said. We'd been flirting around for a while. They show movies in the main ballroom every Sunday night. During *West Side Story*, I pulled him into a storage closet, went down on him."

Kowalski and Proul stared at each other, can't believe what they're hearing. Here's this woman of privilege with the fancy house, expensive cars and clothes, pretending she has a lot of class. But she's standing there dressed to thrill in her sexy red robe sipping orange juice and vodka while talking shit like a street corner hooker. She was as artificial and cheap as the lighting at a Kresge's Dime Store.

Velma could see the faux righteous looks on their faces. She wanted to slap them silly, scrub their faces in the gutter.

"Am I embarrassing you? Well I don't care. I loved every minute of it. But I want those negatives, and I want you to put the fear of God into Germaine and his friends so they can't blackmail me."

"We're homicide cops, lady, not private dicks. Now I know we've done work for you and your husband before."

Velma stood her ground. Eyes cold. Face tightening.

"How many hundreds of dollars have my husband and I paid you the past two years for all those so-called high-class call girls? Most of them down on their luck strippers and hookers. But we never complained, did we?"

Kowalski said, "Now look, Mrs. Turnbull, we—

"Shut up!"

Velma gathered up the photos, stuffed them back into the envelope.

"I'll pay you each one-thousand dollars, two-hundred of it right now."

That got their full attention. No more games with this hot to trot little sweetheart. That was real money talking and they were eager for the score.

Kowalski said, "This Germaine, he got a last name?"

"They don't put last names on name tags."

Proul stood up, walked over to the kitchen sink, took a glass out of a cupboard, picked up the bottle of vodka and poured himself a drink. Velma stared him down.

"You want something else, or are you just practicing?"

Proul gulped down the glass of vodka.

"These other dudes got names?"

Velma walked to the refrigerator and poured herself another glass of orange juice and topped it off with the remains of the bottle of vodka, then turned around to the two cops and smoothed her silk robe down over her hips and thighs with a slow-moving hand, teasing them. The robe wasn't wrinkled. Doing it to get their attention. Velma took a sip of juice. Smirking.

"Names? You know, I was having such a great time, I never bothered to ask. I think one of them said they all used to play football at Redford High."

NINE

Walt's camera shop on Van Dyke was stuck between a dry-cleaners and a donut shop. The window display was chock full of cameras, lights, and darkroom enlargers, some of them new, most of them used and beat up. A middle-aged woman stood behind the counter and munched on a chocolate éclair. Another éclair sat on a napkin by her left hand.

Angelo entered and walked to the counter.

"Can I help you, sir?"

"Yeah, I've got this old German Leica rangefinder I picked up in Germany when the war ended. Haven't used it in years. Stuck a roll of Tri-X black and white in it one night when the wife and I were—"

"You want to know if the camera worked."

Angelo wanted to cut to the chase, but hesitated.

"Walter Robbins the owner?"

That question killed her pleasant expression.

"He died two years ago. I was his wife."

"Sorry to hear that, Ma'am."

"Son, Leica's never break, the camera works, so what you're trying to say is, you took some pics of you and your wife, but you don't want to run that roll of film down to your neighborhood Cunningham Drug Store and take the chance of you and the little lady finding yourselves in an embarrassing situation."

Angelo thought that over a moment.

"That's about the hang of it."

There was the sound of a metallic click behind the lady. Angelo couldn't help but notice. The woman had a scheming smile simmering in her eyes.

"Did you hear that? Take a gaze over my right shoulder. See that camera up on the shelf? That's one of those new Jap Nikon thirty-five-millimeter single lens reflexes. It just took your picture. I've got a remote control hooked up to it with a foot pedal. I don't sell tape recorders, but there's one recording right now. I just turned it on. Don't think I need to show you that. Any questions?"

The old broad with a face clean and pale as a nun had him over a barrel. Getting her game going. Angelo cut to the chase.

"Yeah, how much to develop a roll of film?"

"That Tri-X is one-hundred for a thirty-six exposure. Prints will cost you another fifty each."

Angelo thought that over a couple of clicks.

"Seems a little steep."

The late Walt's wife took no prisoners. The kind of woman who would get mean when someone tried to run her. She took a bite of her éclair and brought her eyes around slowly to meet his.

"They're not your kid's first communion pictures, are they?"

Angelo got the message. He was done acting cute.

"What about eight-millimeter movies?"

"One hundred for a fifty-foot roll, dupes, which most people in your line of work want, are another two-hundred each."

"What about color?"

"You can double that for everything?"

She took the last bite of the éclair, and put pen to paper on an order form.

"You want to give me a name and phone number?"

"I'm just an amateur. Any samples in here I could look at?"

That tore it for the lady, she's lost patience. A ticked-off tone in her voice now.

"See that door you came in? It swings both ways."

Angelo stood there a second, looked her straight in the eye, gave her a wink, then headed for the door.

She finished off the éclair, wiped her mouth on her sleeve and gave her best shot at Angelo as he opened the door.

"Give my best to the boys down at headquarters."

TEN

The house on McGraw was in need of some TLC, but otherwise a fairly solid looking Craftsman that went nicely with the neighborhood. The front lawn was bare of any grass and rutted with tire tracks. Olympia Stadium where the Red Wings played was just up the street on the corner of Grand River. The front lawn brought a premium for parking when it was hockey night in Detroit.

The house was unoccupied and ownership was somewhat sketchy, but Detroit cops used the place for after hour poker games and drinking parties with hookers brought in occasionally for entertainment and romps in the upstairs bedrooms. Today the place was being used for some off the record police interrogation.

Germaine Jefferson sat on an uncomfortable looking wooden chair with his cuffed hands in his lap. He wore his busboy uniform and name tag from the Belle Isle Boat Club. Tears rolled down his cheeks. He'd been slapped around some, but not enough to draw blood or make him silly. Homicide detective

Kowalski stood over him. A half-smoked Lucky Strike was dead between his lips.

"So, Germaine how old are you again?"

"How many times I got to tell you? Nineteen."

"You like feeding your dark meat to prize white pussy, don't you?"

"Fuck you."

That remark brought a couple of hard slaps from Proul, the other hard-nosed detective lingering around.

"Can the wisecracks, asshole. You killed that broad who took pictures of you and your friends doing the nasty with the white woman old enough to be your momma. Didn't you?"

"I don't know no white woman."

Kowalski was wound up. Fire in his eyes.

"Why'd you kill the other broad, the redhead?"

Germaine got the vibe that this-is-no-joke shit they laid on him. Panic set in his eyes.

"I didn't kill no one! What the fuck you talking about?"

Kowalski lit that Lucky Strike and moved in close to Germaine. His lips just inches from Germaine's nose. Kowalski's teeth were stained yellow from nicotine and looked to be the result of some cut-rate dental work. His fat gut was almost touching Germaine's chest.

"Let me spell it out for you. After the little get-together picnic with the ball-busting rich white lady from the Boat Club who likes to slut herself up, you and your buddies figured you'd cash in. Make some extra pocket change to the tune of a hundred grand. Thought it would be as easy as falling off the roof and not hitting the ground. But things didn't go as planned, did they?"

Germaine choked up, crying, he couldn't speak.

Proul moved in for a kill shot question.

"Now Germaine, we can sit here all day, maybe even all night. You can stonewall, and I can sucker punch you till my hands hurt. But I don't wanna do that. You didn't lose your little book of answers. Why don't you come clean? Tell us the truth, we'll put in a good word for you downtown and we can all go home. How 'bout it?"

Now Germaine wasn't a bad kid. Played wide receiver at Redford High. He was a pretty decent one, but not so good at the books. Tried walking on at Wayne State, but that lasted only a week. He turned his books in a few days later.

When he saw Kowalski's gut in his face and that .38 Smith & Wesson police revolver sticking out of Kowalski's holster, Germaine, a kid who had a clean record, was about to make the biggest decision of his life.

Angelo drove south on Van Dyke headed back toward downtown. The old lady at Walt's camera shop had her act together. Her late husband must have showed her the ropes, or maybe it was the other way around. Either way, she had herself covered. There was nothing major illegal about processing stag film. It wouldn't get you any hard time, maybe just a fine; long as the United States Post Office wasn't involved. She played it more than just safe, what with the camera and tape recorder. She had all the bases covered, and probably kept nothing longer than she had to. Being cozy with some of the boys in blue downtown kept the heat off her little operation and she wore that like a feather in her cap.

Angelo noticed a police black and white in the rear-view mirror as it came up on his bumper. When the lights flashed, Angelo pulled over. He rolled down the window just as the uniformed cop approached, and got out his police ID.

The cop looked in the window.

"You John Angelo?"

Angelo showed him his ID.

"They want to see you over at the house on McGraw."

"Who's they?"

"Just relaying the message, pal."

ELEVEN

Police cars were parked all over the front yard of the house on McGraw, and those that couldn't fit were blocking the street. Angelo's Chevy was double parked next to a police cruiser.

Inside, cops in uniforms and suits swarmed the place. Germaine Jefferson was still sitting in that wooden chair. There was a bullet hole in the right side of his cheek, and the exit hole about an inch above his left ear. Kowalski's .38 Smith & Wesson police revolver was clutched in his right hand. His white busboy uniform was now a bloody red. Kowalski lay in a pool of blood at Germaine's feet. There was a bullet hole under his chin and another hole about the same size in the top of his head. Proul was crunched up in the corner with two bullet holes in his face. One was in his left eye, the other just under the nose. His police revolver was in his lap.

A police photographer snapped a series of photos with an old Speed Graphic. A tall, skinny cop in his fifties named Captain O'Dowd stood over the grisly scene with Angelo. O'Dowd spoke low and slow. To him it was just another day at the office, except now two dead cops and a dead black kid were laid out in front of him.

O'Dowd offered Angelo a cigarette.

"Looks like the kid somehow got hold of Kowalski's gun and put one round up under his chin. Before Proul could get his piece out, the kid got him with another round. Proul, on his back, put one in the kid, and then the kid got off one more shot. Probably the round in Proul's eye."

Angelo said, "Who's the kid?"

"Couldn't find any ID other than his name tag, but there's a laundry tag on his uniform shirt that says BIBC."

Angelo said, "Belle Isle Boat Club?"

That brought a smirk to O'Dowd's face.

"Goddamn, you are one smart cookie. How did I ever let you get bumped out of Homicide over to Vice?"

"You pushed me out, remember?"

"How could I forget? Any idea why Bozo and Clarabell were here on their day off?"

"Beats me. Maybe something to do with the two women who turned up dead in my apartment?"

"More than a possibility, but these two hacks wouldn't go out of their way to help their grandma cross the street."

Angelo took a drag on his cigarette.

"That why I'm here, the two dead women?"

"Yeah. You knew both of them… more than casually."

Angelo rolled with that, kept his cool.

"I'm pulling you back into Homicide so give your sex appeal a rest. You're the Lone Ranger on this case. Report only to me. This dead kid doesn't look like an after-hours gun-slinger pulling off stop and robs. But somehow he's tied in with the murder of your two girlfriends."

Angelo let the girlfriends remark pass.

"You're putting a lot of faith in me."

"You were the best homicide cop I had till you went weak in the knees on me. I'm thinking, who's got the most interest in keeping this whole shit-storm from being dumped in the cold case file?"

O'Dowd put an arm around Angelo.

"Here's a chance to redeem yourself. Now go give them hell, Johnny Angel."

TWELVE

Nat Hollywood sat in the living room of a two-story house on West Grand Boulevard. It wasn't really a living room any more. It was the reception area of Motown Records. This wasn't the first time Nat flopped himself in those big black leather sofas. He was here just last month seeking an audition. The entire rear of the house was converted into a recording studio.

Nat imagined himself standing back there in front of a recording microphone, with the smooth sounds of the Funk Brothers, a backup band of local musicians, that would make him sound like the next Smokey Robinson. He had one of Smokey's songs all picked out. Knew it backwards and forwards. Up the right side and down the left.

When a lady approached with a smile on her face, he almost jumped into her lap.

"Nathan?"

"You can call me Nat."

"Okay, Nat. I'm sorry but we don't do open auditions anymore."

Those words were like a kick in Nat's gut. He spit out a weak reply.

"But, Ma'am, you see I been practicing for months. Got all of Smokey's tunes down, even some of Marvin's. I'm ready to go, know what I mean?"

The lady was sympathetic, not wanting to crush his dreams.

"Well, Nat, do you sing with a group, or perform anywhere?"

Nat was quick on his feet.

"I got this boss McIntosh stereo system with Bozak speakers back in my apartment and—"

"There's a recording studio on Grand River called Moonglow. You can rent their sound room, and they'll cut you a demo."

Nat rolled that over in his brain a couple of seconds.

"A demo? How much they charge?"

"I think their rate is one thousand per session and that includes studio musicians."

Nat hadn't anywhere near that amount of cash on hand, but he knew where he could get it.

"Where on Grand River?

THIRTEEN

John Angelo sat in a red velvet chair in the main ballroom of the Belle Isle Boat Club. There were rows and rows of red velvet chairs all facing a silver movie screen that hung from the ceiling at one end of the ballroom. Each chair was methodically placed and the rows were perfect, not a chair out of line. It had the precision of a military cemetery but instead of white crosses, it was a field of red velvet.

Sunday night was movie night, but this was Monday afternoon and sitting in front of him with their chairs turned toward him were five young black men, none more than twenty years old, dressed out in their black slacks and white busboy jackets.

One of the kids spoke.

"None of us knew Germaine that well. He kind of kept to himself."

Another kid piped up.

"He liked to mess around with some of the girls."

That got Angelo's full attention.

"What girls, and what do you mean mess around?"

"Just flirting, stuff like that. They come down on you hard around here you get caught gettin' too friendly with the white girls."

Another kid, the one on the end, with his elbows hung over the back of the chair, eyes glued to the floor spoke.

"There was this one white lady."

That comment brought a round of giggles from the group.

Angelo said, "A lady? She works here?"

The kid on the end said, "No way, man, she a member."

That brought another round of giggles.

"A member? What about this lady member? Are you saying she was messing around with Germaine?"

The kid on the end looked Angelo straight in the eye.

"Not sayin' nothin', but old white ladies don't give us colored boys the time of day, but this one liked to show her shape, seemed to like everyone puttin' eyes on her."

FOURTEEEN

Nat Hollywood parked his Cadillac Fleetwood in the circular drive in front of the Turnbull estate in Grosse Pointe, got out, and hurried to the front door. He didn't even have to knock, for Velma Turnbull was there waiting for him. She wore tight black pedal-pushers, the kind Mary Tyler Moore wore on *The Dick Van Dyke Show*. A black V-neck sweater graced her top and fit like a glove. There was anger in her eyes and voice.

"Well look what the cat dragged in. Get your sorry ass in here."

Nat strolled in, flopped down on her big living room sofa.

"Sorry ass? What you talkin' about?"

"You never gave me a phone number. I don't even know where the fuck you live. Nat Hollywood? Nobody has a last name Hollywood. Operator just laughed when I gave her that name."

"Hey, get over it."

Velma stood over him, all five foot two inches of her, the color of anger rising in her face.

"You said you would take care of everything. Don't worry you said you'll get the negatives and that movie film. No problem. You'll make it all go away."

"So, what's the problem?"

Velma tossed the photos of her and the four young black men onto the sofa next to Nat.

"Here's the problem. These showed up on my doorstep this morning with a demand for a hundred thousand dollars or my husband gets the surprise of his life."

Nat turned that over. Smelling a score that he missed. Why didn't he think of that? He'd been running an errand for her for pocket change when he could have cashed in big with a blackmail scheme like that.

He met Velma at the Big Boy restaurant over on Fort Street last month. Said she had car trouble. He followed her out to her car. That brand new '63 Caddy Coupe Deville. He got in the car. It started right up. Next thing he knows, she's got her hands in his pants. He'd been getting it on with her on Wednesday nights ever since on her overstuffed Simmons Beauty Rest in the upstairs master bedroom while her husband Andy played poker with his rich buddies at the Detroit Athletic Club.

One night she's crying her eyes out. Said she did something real stupid. Hired this gal, good with a camera, and paid her five hundred bucks to put her on film getting real nasty with some young black dudes. Gal named Sophia Martino, a taxi-dancer out at the Woodland Ballroom.

Velma told him she couldn't help herself. Nat could put that all together, because she was insatiable. She made him do things to her that jumped way over that line between kink and debauchery. She gave him a couple hundred to get the movie film and negatives back, and another couple hundred for Sophia to shut her up. Nat looked up at her.

"Bitch said she shot two fifty-foot rolls of color and some black and white stills. She didn't have no film. Couldn't find it nowhere."

Velma stood there, motionless, waiting for Nat to tell her more. But not wanting to hear what might come next. Her eyes were moist and her face as white as a corpse.

"You killed them, didn't you?" It's in the papers."

That made Nat a little slack-jawed, but Nat didn't rile easy.

"Things got heated up just a touch."

Velma took a deep breath and her eyes glinted anger as her face turned red.

"Heated up? You killed two women! You weasel! I bet you pocketed that two hundred you were supposed to pay Sophia."

That riled Nat. He jumped up, kicked over the coffee table.

Startled, Velma backed away.

"Did you kill the two cops and that kid, Germaine, over by the hockey stadium?"

"What cops? I don't know no fucking Germaine. The fuck you talkin' about?"

"It's there in the paper."

Velma threw an afternoon edition of the Detroit Times in his face.

Nat checked the paper, saw the story about the murders out by Olympia. Velma paced back and forth, hands on her hips.

"The kid's name was Germaine Jefferson. He worked at the Boat Club. That's him in the photo with me. The skinny one with the girly tattoos on his arms."

Nat looked at one of the photos of her and the young boys.

"I didn't kill no cops or this kid. Swear to God."

Velma folded her arms across her chest and stood her ground.

"Oh, yeah, well somebody did."

Nat stared at her, thinking *who does this white rich bitch think she is?* He moved close, right up into her face.

"You want me to find these three other dudes. That what you want?"

"You get the movie film and negatives, but you don't kill them. I've got enough blood on my hands already."

"What about the hundred-grand?"

That put a puzzled look on Velma's face. There was no way she could come up with that much money without her husband knowing about it. She could see herself in divorce court, the photos splashed around, the stories in the press. She'd come out of it with a big fat zero.

"Forget about the money. You're a tough guy, just scare the shit out of them."

Nat got up from the sofa and took a step toward her. She took a step back, not sure what he would do.

They locked eyes. Some fear in hers, cold blood in his.

"Okay, but it's gonna cost ya, know what I mean?"

That got Velma's blood up.

"I'm not paying you any more fucking money"

Without a blink, Nat slapped her hard across the face with the open palm of his right hand. It drove her back spread-eagled onto the couch. He'd slapped her hard before, but only on her ass and that was because she asked for it, told him it made her hot. She even let him yank on her hair with both hands. It was all part of their love making.

But now, with a steady drip of blood coming out of both nostrils, she realized that this black lover was someone who could really hurt her bad.

FIFTEEN

John Angelo walked through the lobby of the Belle Isle Boat Club headed for the exit. This was the first time he'd ever been in the place. Drove past it many times when he was cruising around Belle Isle with his high school girlfriend. You could see the rich kids hang by the outdoor pool in the summer while their parents drank cocktails on the decks of their fancy boats.

Angelo had no need to come out to the island anymore. Belle Isle was for kids and families. A ritzy club like this was a place he didn't belong. The downtown YMCA and the Detroit Recreation pool hall were his hangouts when he was young. But his first visit here paid off. The busboys picked out the photo from the membership book of the lady who liked to get friendly with the help. She had a name and a place. Velma Turnbull, and she lived out in Grosse Pointe. It would take him about fifteen minutes to drive there.

Nat Hollywood pulled out of the driveway of Velma's home in Grosse Pointe headed for the Detroit Public Library downtown. It was about a fifteen-minute drive. He flicked on the radio, and punched WCHB, the AM radio station that played Motown and other black artists. He cranked the volume up. The motor on his '56 Fleetwood was running smooth, as smooth as the voice of Mary Wells coming through the dashboard speaker.

He'd had to get serious with Velma back at her place. It took more than a bloody nose for her to come up with the one grand. She fought like hell, so he punched her in the gut, which took the wind out of her sails, but didn't totally convince her.

What brought her around and made her see the light was when he put the squeeze on her pretty little feet. Only size four and a half, she always liked to brag. Always made him kiss and lick them, then suck on her toes before she let him do anything else. He probably crushed some bones before she hollered uncle.

She didn't have the cash so she wrote him a check. And that check was headed right for the Moonglow recording studio. It was all coming together for Nat. He had that photo in his pocket of Velma getting it on with the four dudes. Like he told Velma, all he had to do was take a look at some recent Redford High School yearbooks at the library, find the names of the other three rum-dumbs, and shake them down for the movie film and the negatives.

What he didn't tell Velma was that he had a locked and loaded German Walther P.38 in the glove box. The same pistol his Daddy took as a war prize from a Nazi prisoner at the end of the war. The same gun Nat used to ice Sophia Martino and her redheaded girlfriend. He didn't mean to kill them. But they poked him. Kept jerking his line. Called him a dumb nigger street kid. That if he was any dumber, you'd have to water him twice a week. They didn't let up, so he pulled out the gun, made them strip and get it on with him, then he shot them.

It was a foolproof plan he thought as he pulled into the parking lot of the Detroit Public Library on Woodward. Three dead colored boys floating down the river toward Lake Erie, no one would care, it was Detroit.

He'd keep the movie and the still pics and hold them over Velma's head. Collect a little cash from her now and then till he cut a record and made it big. He'd be missing out on a great piece of ass, but least he wouldn't be sucking on her toes no more.

Angelo rang the bell to the front door of Velma's house. When she opened the door, it wasn't what he expected. The photo at the Belle Isle Boat Club didn't do her justice. She was much prettier, even with the blood that trickled from her nose, the tears in her eyes that ran the mascara down her cheeks and what looked to be a very bad hair day. He noticed her tight black sweater and what looked to be one of those bullet bras that Janet Leigh made famous in the movie *Psycho*.

"Are you with the police?"

Angelo showed her his badge.

"Detroit Homicide."

And with that Velma just lost it. The sobs came in waves as more blood ran out of her nose. She turned away from him and he followed her into the living room.

He noticed those tight black pedal pushers and that nice round bottom, but what caught his attention most was that she sure walked funny in her bare feet, like she was stepping on eggshells.

Nat Hollywood sat at a big oak table in the reading room of the Detroit Public Library. A stack of Redford High School yearbooks was in front of him. He flipped through the pages of the senior section of one book then flipped over to the sports pages to check out the football team photos.

Nat graduated from Mumford High out on Wyoming Boulevard. Cass Tech had the better music program, but he lived right on the border, so Mumford was his only choice. Mumford was mostly white Jewish kids. That's where he learned to fit in with whites, didn't need the cultural refinement that Berry Gordy over at Motown Records demanded. Nat already had it, schooled into him since the ninth grade.

John Angelo left Velma's home with a ton of information. She came clean with him, couldn't stop talking, telling him everything, while wiping the tears from the corners of her eyes with a tissue. Angelo just sat there almost giving her the silent act and let her ramble, while confessing to him with all her heart and soul like she suddenly discovered some inner moral fiber. It might have been an act. A performance worthy of an Academy Award, or at least a nomination.

She showed him the photos. What he noticed first was the bed with the brass headboard, and all those pillows in Sophia Martino's upstairs bedroom. Velma told him about Nat Hollywood. That she only wanted the movie and negatives and never meant that he would murder anyone. She filled him in on Kowalski and Proul and the money she paid each of them to put the fear of God into Germaine.

The woman was a loopy mess. But what Angelo sensed most was that she was more concerned about her husband finding out about this nightmare she created, divorcing her and leaving her penniless, than she was about maybe having to do hard time at the women's prison up in Ionia for conspiracy to commit murder.

As Angelo motored west on Jefferson, with one of those dirty photos in his pocket, he hoped Nat Hollywood was at the library on Woodward, and Angelo would see a black Cadillac Fleetwood in the parking lot. It was starting to snow big wet flakes, not enough to stick to the windshield or road.

He thought about calling for backup, but that would only aggravate the situation. He didn't want to confront this Hollywood guy inside the library. Innocent people could get hurt. No, he'd wait him out in the parking lot. And he was ready for that. So was the Remington pump 12 gauge tucked up under the dash.

SIXTEEN

Velma Turnbull sat naked on the floor in the white tiled shower of her home in Grosse Pointe. The shower was big enough to wash a car, so her tiny frame occupied only one corner. Hot water washed over her, some blood still trickled from her nose, and a black and blue welt on her cheek was getting uglier by the minute.

It had come to this. This high school baton twirler from Terra Haute, Indiana, lost her virginity at age fourteen. It was in the back seat of a '36 Packard owned by one of the rich kids from the country club.

Now at age forty she was about to lose her meal ticket because she couldn't control her lustful urges. Knocking boots with black guys was a line she knew she couldn't cross, but she crossed it anyway. Damn, she sped over it at full throttle. Her husband Andy encouraged and indulged all her fantasies, but racist that he was, fucking black guys was a bridge too far.

That wild night years ago in the Packard was a poisonous lesson. What she learned was that her body was the ticket out of poverty. Countless young men from the university, soldiers heading off to war, men she'd meet at dances and in bars, plied her with money and gifts.

It was a scam that worked. Kept her in nice clothes, a half-way decent used car. She never had to walk the streets or stand on a street corner. She had too much class, or so she thought, for that. Enough class to land that trust fund baby Andy Turnbull, thirteen years her junior. And now, with Andy due home from the condo in Tampa in a couple of days, she had better come up with a new plan.

Angelo sat in his unmarked car in the parking lot of the Detroit Public Library's main branch on Woodward Avenue. He guessed right, for Nat Hollywood's black '56 Fleetwood was parked in the row just ahead. Nat would come out of the library with some names and what he was looking for, or he'd come out with a sour look on his face wondering what the fuck to do next. But either way, he'd come out of that library and jump in his Caddy.

The snow showers had stopped, and the sun peeked through the clouds now and then. Angelo kept his eyes glued on the Fleetwood. Back working homicide now, if only for a while, he wanted to tidy this all up, put the cuffs on Hollywood, and find out what went down at his apartment. Why were Sophia and Lil' Red naked in the bed? Did he bloody up their faces with his fists before or after he put a couple of rounds into them? That was just for starters.

Sooner than expected a black man of about twenty-five came walking through the parking lot. Before he got thirty feet from the Cadillac Angelo knew it was Nat Hollywood. You couldn't miss the black leather pants. Nat wasn't smiling, neither was he looking pissed. His facial expression was more of a shit-eating smirk. Angelo yanked the 12 gauge from under the dash, and stepped out of the car. He kept the shotgun in his right hand and let it hang from his side out of sight, so Hollywood couldn't spot it.

Angelo walked toward the Caddy. When Hollywood got to the driver side door, Angelo hollered.

"You Nat Hollywood?"

Nat put his right hand on the door handle and his eyes on Angelo.

"Who's askin'?"

Angelo brought up the shotgun so Hollywood could see it.

"Detroit Police. You're under arrest."

There was a tinge of panic on Hollywood's face as he ripped open the door of the car and jumped behind the wheel. He started the car, threw it in reverse and backed up right toward Angelo.

Angelo jumped out of the way of the speeding car and sprinted to the driver side window. The window exploded into pieces from a gunshot from inside the car. Angelo pointed the barrel of the shotgun into the opening and saw the Walther P.38 pointed at his face. He didn't hesitate. He let Hollywood have it with two rounds. Hollywood got off one more shot that shattered the windshield. The Caddy lurched back for another twenty feet and slammed into Angelo's car, then came to a halt, the rear tires burning rubber before the engine cut out.

Angelo rushed to the blown-out window and set the barrel of the shotgun on the windowsill. He stood there a few seconds, motionless. Suddenly it was like the world went silent. He couldn't hear the sound of the rush of traffic on Woodward or the music that blared from the Caddy's radio. He looked to the sky at birds fluttering from tree to tree, and he couldn't hear them. Fifteen years he'd worked homicide, and this was the first time he ever shot anyone. It all came back to him now. The blood and guts he saw during the war as a combat MP; that one deserter who shot himself in the face. Another hanged himself with his socks.

All those years working homicide and seeing those dead bodies knifed, shot, strangled, beaten. The nightmares that followed had haunted him ever since. Now he could feel the winter chill in the air. When the world came alive again, it was the Cadillac's radio he heard first.

Angelo opened the car door. One round had raked the flesh off Hollywood's face and the other round caught him square in the chest. Angelo pulled open Hollywood's coat and saw a ripped-out yearbook football team photo, and three other pages of senior photos. Hollywood had found what he was looking for. What gave Angelo some comfort at the moment was that he probably saved three black kids lives whose only crime, and it wasn't a crime, was giving a white woman, old enough to be their mother, a kinky fantasy she wanted brought to life. But that comfort only lasted a flash in time.

Angelo pulled Hollywood's wallet from the back pocket and saw the name Nathan Cain on his Michigan driver's license. There was also that personal check for one thousand dollars that

Nat scammed off Velma Turnbull. He put Nat's wallet back, but for some reason, he folded that check and slipped it in his own pocket. He took one more look at the bloody, dead face of Nat Hollywood, reached for the radio knob and turned off Smokey Robinson.

SEVENTEEN

The Saturday before Memorial Day, 1963 was sunny and warm. Row after row of headstones were decorated with small American flags at Detroit's Woodmere Cemetery on Fort Street. John Angelo stood in front of one of the headstones. It was the final resting place for one U.S. Army soldier. The date of birth was 1930 and the date of death 1950. The place of death was Korea. The name on the headstone read Salvatore Martino. That photo he saw back in December at Sophia's house, the one that resembled him when he was young was her son. He'd discovered that when he was looking for next of kin.

Angelo walked a few yards to two freshly dug graves beside which sat two plain metal coffins. They contained the bodies of Sophia and Lil' Red. He'd come up empty looking for any living relatives for either of them. They didn't do burials in the dead of winter so Angelo paid to keep them on ice until the weather got warmer. He also paid for the coffins and other burial services. He tapped into his slush fund across the river in Windsor for the cash.

He thought about taking up a collection at the Empress Burlesque and the Woodland Ballroom, but decided this would all be on him. There weren't any other mourners, just him with his thoughts of guilt and regret. Nobody here to say anything about them but what was there to say? Two women doing the best they could in the ugly world in which they lived.

That night Angelo made his usual rounds on his vice beat. Nothing was out of the ordinary on this late May evening. The temperature hovered in the mid-seventies and the humidity was low. The stifling heat of July and August were weeks down the road. And as Angelo drove Woodward Avenue, he kept the driver and passenger side windows down so he could feel the cool southeast breeze blowing in off the Detroit River.

His job was to keep the lid on, and that's what he did. His world of hookers, pimps, pushers, and strippers wasn't going away no matter what he did. He could be a hard ass, but he learned that was a dead end from his years in homicide.

Angelo made his way over to Hastings and Piquette streets, near G.M. Fisher Body Plant #21. The same plant that made Nat Hollywood's '56 Fleetwood, now being scrapped for parts in a junkyard over on Dixie Highway. Black girls liked to work the corners about a block from the plant from late May to early August. That was when the plant put on an afternoon shift that got out around midnight. The girls could earn in one week what they might take home in a month any other time of the year.

Angelo pulled his unmarked Ford sedan over to the curb one block west of the plant. There were a group of girls hanging near a new Cadillac Coupe Deville chatting up the driver. The door opened and out stepped a tall, about 6 feet 5, and maybe a little dangerous, black man. He wore a black sharkskin suit, lavender shirt, and skinny black tie. He walked back to where Angelo was parked, his pointed toe black leather shoes with metal heel plates clicked across the sidewalk. His gaze wandered over to Angelo.

He looked in the window.

"What's happening, boss?"

"Are your girls age appropriate, Winston?"

"Hey man, you know I always doin' the right thing. Got a new girl, name's Ruby, she can do you, if you want, I can call her over. She the one with the blonde wig and red dress."

Angelo looked to the corner and saw a gorgeous black girl in a beautifully coifed blonde wig.

"Winston, you pay for all those fancy outfits?"

"Damn straight. My girls are high class. Nobody in all of Detroit lookin' better than my girls."

"Keep them clean, Winston."

Winston dropped a twenty into Angelo's lap.

Angelo pulled away from the curb and headed for Woodward Ave toward the National Burlesque. The National was the high end, if you could call it that, of the strip joints downtown. The Stone Burlesque fit somewhere in the middle, maybe one peg up from the Empress. All of them probably on their last dying dance, but they kept hanging on. About the only other place you could see a naked woman was at the Melody Art

Theater on Michigan Avenue out near Garden City. And they only showed those silly bouncing beach balls and boobs nudist flicks.

Angelo stood in the back of the National. The place was packed with your typical younger crowd, but this time decked out in t-shirts, Bermuda shorts, and tennis shoes.

The bouncer, a ratty-looking guy named Punch, approached Angelo.

"What do you think of the new girl, Destiny?"

Angelo just nodded.

Destiny was dancing to the song *Diamonds Are A Girl's Best Friend*.

She had on a blonde wig, tight red satin dress, and white gloves that reached all the way up her arms. Under all that movie star façade was one Velma Turnbull. Velma was doing a Marilyn Monroe impersonation from the movie *How To Marry A Millionaire*. Marilyn wasn't one year in the ground, but the act was going over like gangbusters with the crowd. Things didn't work out so well for Velma. Husband Andy divorced her all right, but the pics weren't what did her in. Seems Andy Turnbull came back to Grosse Pointe with a twenty-two-year old former cheerleader from Florida State University.

Velma managed to skate on any conspiracy charges. It helped that Angelo tore up that check she wrote to Nat Hollywood. Those negatives and eight-millimeter film were out there somewhere. Angelo was never able to track them down, but it was no skin off his back. And watching Velma up there on stage taking if all off, it probably didn't bother her, other than not getting one dime from her kinky film career.

Punch slipped a twenty into Angelo's pocket.

"For an old broad with a body like that, she's been packing them in, three shows a night and the carpet don't have to match the drapes."

Angelo didn't say anything, he just gave a little shrug.

When the song wound down Velma slithered around the stage only in a red G-string. And when the song ended and that G-string came off, those young boys couldn't get enough of a forty-year old woman shaved like that down there.

Angelo finished his rounds that night and pocketed almost a hundred bucks. It was a nice little addition to his account in Windsor that he socked away for retirement. After clocking out at Police Headquarters around 2 a.m. he stopped at a White Castle on Michigan Avenue to get a cup of coffee. Sitting there at the counter, drinking his coffee black, he thought about the last five months. And none of those thoughts were pleasant. Working Vice was better than Homicide, but not by much. Less blood and guts, and at least you got to interact with people getting on with life, even though most of that life was illegal. Eighteen years on the force, he reminded himself, two more years he could clock out for good and collect his pension. Two years? He could do that standing on his head. Move to Florida. Get a condo, learn to play golf, maybe meet an honest woman.

The front door of the White Castle opened and in walked a young woman who looked to be about eighteen years old.

She had long blonde hair pulled back in a pony tail, and one of those peaches and cream complexions with big blue eyes that seemed to be the M. O. for all those rich girls out in Birmingham and Bloomfield Hills. Throw a stick down Woodward Avenue between 12 Mile Road and Square Lake Road and you'd hit a couple thousand of them.

She had on navy blue toreador pants, tennis shoes, and a white blouse cut low enough in the front to reveal just a peek of cleavage.

She sat a couple of stools down from Angelo and placed what looked to be a textbook on the counter then reached in her purse for a pack of Chesterfields. She had smoked her last one, so the pack was empty. She crumpled it up and tossed it into a waste basket behind the counter a good ten feet from where she sat. Angelo noticed.

"Nice, got a jump shot to go along with that?"

She smiled at him, but didn't speak. The waitress came over and the girl ordered a hamburger and chocolate malt.

Angelo moved to the stool next to her and placed his pack of Chesterfields next to her book.

"Here, we smoke the same brand."

She smiled again and took one of his cigarettes.

"Thank you."

Angelo got out his Zippo and lit her up, his eyes on the title of that book in front of her on the counter.

"Human Anatomy? That a best seller?"

She laughed a little at that.

"Only for the professor who wrote it."

"You're a college student?"

"Wayne State. I'm in the nursing program."

Angelo turned that over, keeping quiet eyes on her.

"What's a nursing student doing hanging out at a White Castle at 2:30 on a Sunday morning?"

She seemed to take some offense at that as she took a long drag on her cigarette.

"I'm twenty-one. Any law against getting a burger and malt?"

"Sorry, no offense."

"None taken. I'm pulling an all-nighter."

"A what?"

"I have a human anatomy final on Tuesday after Memorial Day. I've been booking it since 6 o'clock, just came in here for a little break."

"When do you sleep?"

"All day Sunday. Then on Memorial Day, a friend and I are heading over to the beach in Saugatuck on Lake Michigan."

"I hear that's quite the college party town."

She looked at him long and steady, and being cool drew another drag on the Chesterfield then blew out a couple of near perfect smoke rings. Almost too perfect for someone her age.

"So, what do you do? I bet you're a cop."

That surprised him. For some reason not many strangers took him for a cop.

"Cop? No, I'm in sales, auto parts."

"Anybody buying auto parts this time of night?"

She was a little too clever for her own good, but Angelo played along.

"You never know who might walk in that door."

She stubbed out her cigarette in an ash tray, just as the waitress put her burger and malt on the counter.

She turned toward him and played with the top two buttons on her blouse, teasing him to take a look. He could see she wasn't wearing a bra.

"Okay, Mr. Auto parts guy. I'm going to finish my little snack and then… is there somewhere or someplace we could go? Maybe you could help me with my… human anatomy."

EIGHTEEN

Angelo drove east on Jefferson headed toward his apartment and thought about Miss run around Sue back at the White Castle. He'd flashed his badge and checked her ID. Her name was Sylvia Coyne, was all of nineteen and lived in Corktown, just off Trumbull Avenue. She told him her folks worked the graveyard shift at Dodge Main and laid it on thick about a horrible childhood, like that was an excuse for doing tricks. But Angelo wasn't buying any of it. She wouldn't give him the name of a pimp. Said she worked alone.

Angelo paid for her burger and chocolate malt, had the waitress stick them in a take-out bag, then put Sylvia in a cab, and gave the cabby thirty bucks and told him to drive her home. He also told the cabby that if she got doll-eyed and came on to him, and asked for thirty for a tumble in the back seat, he was to drive her straight to police headquarters. He gave Sylvia one of his cards and told her if the cabby got out of line, that she should call him pronto. The look on both their faces said they got the message.

Angelo parked his car in front of his apartment, walked up the sidewalk, stuck his key in the lock and entered. All that busted up furniture from last winter was replaced with new stuff he had delivered from the Art Van store. He even had that Murphy bed ripped out of the wall in the bedroom and bought one of those new Queen Size mattresses. And there was somebody on that mattress when he strolled into the bedroom, but she wasn't any Queen. It was no surprise to Angelo, because she'd been there every night for a while. Velma Turnbull flicked on the nightstand lamp and rolled over to him. Without makeup she looked older than her forty years and her dark black hair had a few strands of gray around the temples. She pulled the covers up over her bare breasts, squinted at him, and flicked off the lamp.

"There's a leftover TV dinner in the fridge. You can heat it up if you want."

NINETEEN

The wind sailed through Skip Ten Eyck's blonde crew cut hair. For a city kid, his face was tan, an orange tan, the result of a bottle of cheap self-tanner that just came on the market. He wore a powder blue Ban-Lon shirt, white Levi's and a pair of leather sandals with old tire tread for soles. He couldn't pronounce what those sandals were called. His cousin from San Diego sent him a pair. And the Beach Boys were singing about them on the car radio. He loved the Beach Boys, especially *Surfin' U.S.A.,* almost as much as he loved his 1962 Corvette convertible.

It was white with red interior, a four-speed on the floor and Chevy's 283 V-8. He'd read that G.M. was coming out with a new model soon. This would be the last of this breed so he babied it, but wasn't shy about putting pedal to the metal while cruising Woodward Avenue looking for an XKE or Dodge Hemi to shut down.

But he wasn't on Woodward Avenue this sunny Memorial Day morning, 1963. He was headed west on Interstate-96;

destination Lake Michigan. Next to him sat a top-blessed, leggy young turn-on with bedroom eyes by the name of Laurel Gray. Laurel was twenty-two and grew up on a wheat farm in rural Saskatchewan to Ukrainian immigrants with a surname that used up just about every letter in the alphabet. When someone said she looked like the Hollywood actress Gloria Grahame in an old Humphrey Bogart flick on TV she took the name of Gloria's character, Laurel Gray. Liked it so much it was the name that went on her fake Michigan driver's license. She had a round cute face like Gloria with the innocence of a girl who still believed in Santa Claus. Laurel wore short-shorts, like the song a few years back, and smeared Coppertone Dark Tanning Oil over her long limbs. She was wearing the top to a yellow two-piece bathing suit and a floppy straw hat with a brim the size of a spare tire, held in place with a leather string drawn tight under her chin. Her raven black hair reached the small of her back. A pair of Ray-Ban Wayfarer sunglasses capped her look.

Skip was known as Paper Boy and considered himself the luckiest guy in Metro Detroit. He'd worked hard for what he had. By age nineteen he had the most profitable Detroit Times delivery route in the city. He covered all his hometown of Garden City, Westland, Wayne, and half of Dearborn Heights; he had ten neighborhood kids on their Schwinn's pedaling their asses off.

Skip put that in the rearview mirror when he turned twenty. And now at age twenty-three he was into more profitable deliveries to the likes of Grosse Pointe, Birmingham, Bloomfield Hills, Ann Arbor and East Lansing. If you wanted to smoke a little reefer, he delivered. Wanted some live girl entertainment for a frat party or your own one-on-one party, Skip delivered. Skip looked over at Laurel next to him. Today he was going to party hard with the college kids, maybe even scare up some new business. As the Beach Boys sang on the radio, Laurel reached over and flicked off the music. Skip hollered.

"Hey! What the fuck you doing?"

Laurel replied with a generous amount of attitude.

"You know I hate the Beach Boys. Besides, they're copycats."

She flicked the radio back on. The Beach Boys still singing *Surfin' U.S.A.*

Laurel said, "Forget about the words and just listen to the melody. Hear that? The music's dead on Chuck Berry's *Sweet Little Sixteen*. How much you want to bet Chuck's pissed that five white boys stole his song? Yeah, Chuck won't be rocking on Bandstand in Philadelphia P.A, he'll be hiring a lawyer and suing their asses off in Califor-ni-a."

Skip shot her a puzzled look. Skip had a few rocks in the head and Laurel wasn't any dopey girlfriend. She was ten times smarter than he was. She knew it, and he knew it. Laurel wasn't one of the girls he hired out, or just some floozy who knew how to shake her ass that he picked up for a weekend fling. She kept the Paper Boy's head above water.

Skip said, "You're crazy."

Laurel removed the Ray-Bans, her dark Eastern European eyes smoldering in an icy unforgettable stare as she locked eyes with him. Skip got the message. He learned from day one she was a woman with whom you better watch your step. Skip tuned the radio to a different channel playing a sappy, Perry Como tune, and took the Saugatuck exit off U.S.-31.

TWENTY

John Angelo opened the living room drapes of his apartment and let in the morning light. One block off Jefferson, he could see the sun reflect off the river, and the Uniroyal plant. It was going to be a warm Memorial Day said the TV weatherman, with a high in the low eighties. Angelo sat on the sofa with a cup of coffee. The Indy 500 race would be on ABC's *Wide World of Sports* in a couple of hours, and he looked forward to that on his day off.

Velma Turnbull was rooting around in the kitchen looking for something to eat. Angelo wondered if she'd ever be able to fix something herself. Only thing she was good at in the kitchen was peeling back the tin foil on the corner of a Swanson TV dinner. She'd been living with Angelo for two months. Kindness, empathy, or stupidity on his part? Sophia and Lil' Red would still be alive if it wasn't for her.

Somehow, he let that pass. Did he forgive her? No, he didn't. Most of the time she kept to herself, and he'd give her the silent treatment when she got on his nerves, but the sex was there morning, afternoon, or night. He'd nudge her, she'd nudge him. They didn't keep score.

Velma settled on a bowl of dry Sugar Frosted Flakes since there wasn't any milk in the refrigerator, and plopped down next to Angelo on the sofa. She had on a white terrycloth robe and nothing underneath. She sat around most of the day like that watching game shows and Soaps on the TV. He wondered if she did the same thing when she lived in that big house in Grosse Pointe. But if she got bored with all that fancy stuff, she could always drive to the club on Belle Isle for lunch, or swim in the indoor pool, or sit in the steam room. Maybe get a massage. Or to change it up, have lunch at the Roostertail restaurant on the river, then take a squash lesson at the Detroit Athletic Club downtown. But that life was gone. Living here in a one-bedroom apartment with a $8,000 a year vice cop was about the best she could do. She didn't complain a lot; missed that '63 Cadillac Coupe Deville, though. She had to settle for a 1960 Ford Falcon and the clothes on her back in the divorce settlement. She wasn't looking forward to a Detroit summer without air conditioning driving around in that heap of a car. She bitched about the hand crank roll down windows.

Velma was quiet, hadn't said as much as a good morning, just sat there with that bowl of Frosted Flakes in her lap and shoveled them into her mouth with an oversized soup spoon. She looked over at Angelo, stopped eating and gave him a long look.

He'd seen that look before, usually when she got the urge, her eyes holding on him, with a smile as coy as the Mona Lisa. He visualized her tearing off her bathrobe and Frosted Flakes flying all over and into that new sofa he paid three hundred bucks for at Art Van. They'd done it in bed, on the floor, in the shower, even in the kitchen, but never on the sofa, and he wanted to keep it that way.

She finally said something.

"I'm seeing someone else."

Angelo didn't expect that. She had told him before she shacked up with him that she had managed to get a grip on the lust in her loins and living out her fantasies. Swore off younger guys, or so she said. This wasn't the first time he got dumped, but it was the first time a stripper cut him loose.

"Anybody I know?"

"Someone I met at the Belle Isle Boat Club."

"Married?"

"With two grown kids."

"Well… at least you're not robbing the cradle."

She didn't take that as a joke.

"He's fifty-five, a partner in a big law firm over in the Penobscot building. He handled my divorce."

Angelo wanted to laugh, but held it back. She's fucking the lawyer that got her a beat-up Ford with hand crank windows, no air conditioning, and zip in the way of alimony. Now that's gratitude. He looked at her a long moment, watched her munch those dry as a desert Frosted Flakes.

"This mean you'll be moving out?"

"He's setting me up in an apartment across the river in Windsor. It's a real nice place, right on the water. Got a great view."

"He getting you a cook and a maid, too?"

Velma wasn't appreciating Angelo's sarcasm at this time in the morning, but she kept her feelings in check.

"I'm going to be dancing at a new club in Windsor. They have a cover charge and serve alcohol. With tips I'll be able to rake in five times more in a week than I do now at the National."

Angelo was at a loss for words, but talk wasn't in their makeup. They got it on all the time, but never were close. And when they were physically spent, they lit cigarettes and smoked in silence.

Velma set the half-finished bowl of Frosted Flakes on the floor, then looked at Angelo with a trace of a smile.

"I appreciate all you've done for me these last couple of months. I really mean that."

Angelo saw what was coming next. He saw it the minute she set that bowl of cereal on the floor and started giving him those fidgety little moves. It was written in her bedroom eyes and all over her polished and clean face. That robe was coming off and she'd show him the nice goodies. They were going to break in that sofa. What the hell, sex was how their relationship began, might as well end it the same way.

Later, Angelo helped Velma load up her Ford Falcon with the two pieces of luggage she had and wished her well. She gave him a hug and asked him for one last favor. Would he track down that eight-millimeter film of her that was still out there? She didn't care about the still pics or negatives, but that film haunted her. Angelo told her he'd do what he could, and get back to her. She gave him the address of her new digs in Windsor then drove off.

When he got back into his apartment the Indy 500 had started. Parnelli Jones and Jim Hurtubise were dueling for the lead on the first two laps. Then the phone rang.

Angelo picked up.

"Yeah, this is Angelo."

He listened, and didn't like what he heard on the other end of the line. It was the Chief of Homicide.

TWENTY-ONE

Skip Ten Eyck's Corvette cruised Saugatuck's main drag. Traffic was bumper to bumper with cars filled with college aged kids. And the sidewalks jammed with white-bread boys and girls wearing shorts and t-shirts with logos from just about every college in Michigan.

Skip looked at Laurel.

"Know what? This reminds me of that movie. All those college kids on spring break in Florida."

Laurel gave him a weary yawn.

"*Where the Boys Are.*"

That clicked with Skip.

"Yeah, just like the song by Connie Stevens."

"Connie Francis."

"Huh?"

Laurel blew out an exasperated breath.

"Connie Francis sang *Where the Boys Are,* Connie Stevens plays Cricket Blake on the TV show *Hawaiian Eye* and sang that dopey song *Kookie, Kookie, Lend Me Your Comb.*"

Skip churned that over in his brain a hair-second.

"*77 Sunset Strip?*"

"You got it, Ace."

Skip thought he was on a roll with the trivia.

"Connie Stevens. She is one hot little blonde. She played Kookie's girlfriend, right?"

Laurel rolled her eyes. Top-to-bottom, brains wise, Skip was a guy where the game ran past him years ago. If it wasn't for her, he'd still be peddling a Schwinn on his paper route, not driving a boss '62 'Vette. She was the brains that put him in the chips. Laurel cranked up the radio, moved her bottom and bobbed her head to the beat of Leslie Gore's *It's My Party,* looked over at Skip and flashed him one of her rare smiles.

"Find a place to park. I need to eat."

The James Scott Memorial Fountain on Detroit's Belle Isle was surrounded by black and white police cars and roped off with yellow police tape. A police photographer snapped pictures of a dead young female lying on the ground next to the fountain. Her hair was blonde, pulled back in a pony tail. She wore blue toreador slacks and a white top.

Chief O'Dowd and Angelo sat in the back seat of a police black and white. O'Dowd looked out at the fountain.

"Some old folks out for a walk saw her floating out by the wall near one of the lion heads. Shook them up. Probably the first time they'd ever seen a dead body other than in a funeral home, let alone one with her throat slit ear to ear."

Angelo held the water logged business card he gave the girl at the White Castle on Saturday night.

"You're pulling me back in, putting me on this case, all because you pulled this out of her pocket."

"Yeah, that's the gist of it. What other reason could there be? After all, in the last five months you've been connected with the deaths of one stripper, a taxi-dancer, now a hooker that looks all of seventeen. And you shot the hell out of the suspect in the first two murders before ballistics had a chance to match his weapon. Lucky for you, it did. You wrapped that case up nice and neat, so I'm thinking who better to pull a rabbit out of the hat on this one."

Angelo twirled his business card in his fingers.

"I don't want anyone on this with me unless I ask."

"You never ask. I know… you don't want anyone fucking this up. Start with the home address she gave you then corner the cabby."

"Basic Investigative 101, huh?"

O'Dowd threw Angelo a not too pleasant look.

"Get the fuck out of the car. You're the magician, so go do your magic."

"Where's your bushy, bushy, blonde hairdo?"

The question was directed to Skip Ten Eyck. He sat at a table in the Coral Gables Restaurant in Saugatuck with his hand wrapped around a bottle of Pabst Blue Ribbon. Laurel Gray had her hands full with a hamburger and a Coke. The air was lousy with cigarette smoke and the place was packed with college kids as the noise bounced off the walls. The girl asking the question was Tinker Bell cute with short pixie cut hair. She wore a tight pair of pedal pusher jeans and a t-shirt that read *Surfboards by Dewey Webber.* She sat with three other girls all about the same age. Eighteen, maybe nineteen.

Skip leaned over to their table.

"What?"

She pointed at his feet.

"I like your Huarache sandals. You got a surfboard on top of your car?"

The girl and her friends giggled. That's how you say it, Skip thought. On the Beach Boys song, it sounded like wurocchi, or something like that. He thought about asking her to spell it out, but didn't want to seem dumb.

Skip said, "Where do you go to school?"

"We all go to Western in Kalamazoo, where do you go?"

Skip had to think of a school. If he picked one in Michigan she might ask if he knew so and so, what dorm he lived in; or he'd trip up somehow.

"Just graduated from Duke in South Carolina."

"Wow. Isn't Duke in North Carolina?"

Skip was about to stutter out a few words but couldn't think of anything to say. He looked over at Laurel for help, but she had a look on her face that said, you dug the hole, dipshit, you climb out of it.

The girl looked at her friends, cooking something up; like they had a plan.

"Hey surfer boy, if you buy us some beer, we know this great party at a house on the beach."

TWENTY-TWO

John Angelo walked up to the front porch of a house off Trumbull. The same address listed on the license that Sylvia Coyne showed him Saturday night at the White Castle just before he put her in a cab. He'd run down the cab driver who told him this is where he dropped her. The cabby was an old guy pushing sixty, seemed honest enough and smart enough to not do bad stuff to the girl. Angelo believed him, but what concerned him now was what would happen when he knocked on the front door. Would a nice couple maybe his age with a daughter who ran away answer? He'd have to tell them she was dead. Watch them break down and cry. He'd been there done that all the years he worked Homicide. When a burly guy with a big belly wearing a sleeveless t-shirt opened the door, he didn't feel much better. Angelo showed him his badge.

"Does Sylvia Coyne live here?"

The guy took a swig from a can of Stroh's.

"Sylvia who?"

"Sylvia Coyne. Do you know a Sylvia Coyne?"

"Ain't nobody by that name here."

"She has blonde hair, usually wears it in a pony tail. Was wearing blue toreador pants. Real pretty girl, about nineteen, twenty. Have you seen anyone in the neighborhood who matches that description?"

"No, and any chick lookin' like that come walking through this neighborhood, I'd notice. Anything else? I wanna get back to the race."

Angelo could hear the TV in the living room and the Indy 500 he was missing.

"No. Thanks for your time."

Angelo got back in his car and sat there a moment. He should've driven the girl himself, walked her up to the front door, exposed her scam and the phony ID she'd shown him, then taken her downtown. Had he done that she might still be alive. Guilt was getting to be a bad habit with him these past few months. He needed to think, clear his mind. He was only a couple of blocks from the Anchor Bar up on Michigan Avenue. He decided to get a drink, and ask if anyone recognized the girl from his description. Maybe he'd get lucky. And he might catch the last couple laps of the race.

As Lake Michigan beach cottages go, it was more like a mansion. The entire front of the house was wall to wall windows that fronted the lake. College kids sat on towels in the sand and drank beer. Others played in the two-foot waves that rolled in to the shore. Two guys on surfboards tried to ride the waves but weren't having much luck. Except for the half a dozen girls who'd taken off their bikini tops, it could've been a scene right out of the movie *Gidget* with Sandra Dee.

Inside the house a makeshift three-piece band with two kids on Fender guitars and one banging on a set of Ludwig drums butchered an old Jerry Lee Lewis tune. Beer was everywhere. Some kids had a can or bottle in each hand. Several had a joint in their mouth, puffing away with a sleepy-eyed look, thanks to Laurel Gray behind her Wayfarers and straw hat, who worked the crowd handing out perfectly rolled reefers from her oversized beach bag at ten bucks a pop.

Upstairs in one of the bedrooms, Skip Ten Eyck sat on an oversized bed with the girl who wore the *Surfboards by Dewey Webber* t-shirt. The shirt was now on the floor. She toyed with her bra straps. Maybe she'd take it off, maybe she wouldn't. She was higher than a month of Sundays and her speech slurred.

"You don't surf, do you?"

Skip had a comfortable relaxed expression, eyes glued on her cleavage.

"Does it matter?"

The girl rolled her eyes and giggled.

"I want me a real surfer boy. Just tell me you're a real surfer boy."

The bedroom door opened and in walked Laurel. She latched the door behind her and walked over to the bed, placed her bag on the floor, sat down and took off her hat and sunglasses. The girl looked at Laurel, patient for a couple of seconds.

"Are you his girlfriend?"

Laurel hung her long legs seductively over the edge of the bed as she petted the girl's face with her smoldering dark eyes.

"Honey, we're all Skip's girlfriend."

"They stole the fucking race from that Brit, Jim Clark. Parnelli Jones' car was leaking oil like a sieve, and they didn't black flag him, so he took the checkered flag and Clark came in second. I tell ya, there oughta be a law."

The man behind that rant was Chuck, the bartender this Memorial Day at the Anchor Bar. He was bending John Angelo's ear while Angelo nursed a Canadian Club on the rocks.

"Hey, Chuck, have you seen a young girl in here, blonde hair, pony tail, cute little figure, goes by the name Sylvia Coyne?"

"The name sounds familiar. Does she lug around a bag of school books?"

"Yeah. That could be her. She's been in here?"

"Not in the last month. I chased her out one night. Thought she could peddle reefers to the crowd after a twilight double header. Fred might know more."

"Fred off today?"

"Fred quit three weeks ago."

Quit?" He's worked here for ten years. What happened?"

"Nothing. He just up and walked out. Said he had a better gig somewhere else. Might have had something to do with his wife leaving him and moving back to Port Huron."

"You got Fred's address, phone number?"

"Won't do no good. I tried calling him and it was disconnected. Drove over to where he lived on Shaffer, but he'd cleared out. Landlord said he still owed a month's rent."

"You said Fred might know more about the girl."

"One time we pulled a shift together, she came in, opened one of those college books, got a little flirty with Fred. He later told me he was gonna help her with her homework but he was just kidding around, I think."

Angelo downed the last of his Canadian Club, dropped a five on the bar and got up to leave.

"Thanks, Chuck. You hear anything, let me know."

As Angelo left, Chuck hollered at him.

"If you find out where's he's at, give us a call. He's got a week's pay owed him."

Angelo headed back to his apartment. He took Michigan Avenue east through downtown. It was dusk and the street lights were coming on. Traffic was almost zilch. He passed by the Empress Burlesque. The marquee lights were dark but he could still see the billboards of the girls dressed in their skimpy outfits. It reminded him of better times when he was working Vice, but then the two murders brought him back to reality, and now the brutal murder of the girl he could have saved at the White Castle was a constant ache in his gut.

He told himself he'd get a good night's sleep. Wake up fresh and full of energy. Get a jump on this case. He wasn't going to let it get dumped in the cold file, not on his watch. Angelo took a left on Jefferson and drove east. The air was dead calm, and so was the river as it reflected the glow of city lights from Detroit and Windsor.

Skip and Laurel left Saugatuck just after sunset and headed east on I-96 back to Detroit. Laurel had a small blanket tucked under her head against the car window and was trying to sleep, but wasn't having any luck. Skip jabbered in her ear the first hour about this and that: the beach, the girls, how they scored close to a grand on dope. Laurel managed to shut him up, and now she pretended to sleep to keep him quiet. He could grate on you, and she thought about dumping him to strike out on her own again, but the pay was steady, he bought her nice clothes and didn't pimp her out or push her to strip at bachelor or frat parties. It was a way better life than anything back in Saskatchewan.

At age fifteen Laurel won a ribbon as runner-up for Miss Hometown Moose Jaw. Sixteen found her pregnant. She abandoned the baby girl with her mother three weeks after giving birth and joined a traveling carnival in Thunder Bay, Ontario running the Tilt-A-Whirl.

Six months later she was dealing three-card Monte in a tent shared with an old woman fortune teller. Skip pulled her out of that job after she scammed him for ten bucks during the Polish Festival in Boyne Falls, Michigan.

He told her he liked her style. Said she was pretty. Skip was a talker and could lay it on thick. Promised her the world, but he wasn't the sugar daddy she was looking for. Laurel saw through his bullshit, followed him to Detroit and found her niche. She could roll the most perfect joints at record clip. They nicknamed her Lady Fingers. And most important, this girl with the fast fingers and a gift with numbers kept all the books.

TWENTY-THREE

Angelo took the Port Huron exit off I-94 and headed for an apartment building downtown. He'd found an address for Fred's ex-wife, Carla. She was still using his last name, Nowak. If Fred was carrying a torch for her, maybe he'd get lucky and find him there. Angelo never met her, but she had quite the rap sheet. Prostitution, possession of drugs, and armed robbery. Fred met her when he was cranking out eight-millimeter stag films years ago. She was one of his performers and must be close to forty years old.

When she opened the door of her apartment, he was shocked to see what looked to be a woman knocking on sixty. She was rail thin with dark, deep set eyes and stringy salt and pepper gray hair. As soon as Angelo identified himself, she gave him a warm smile.

"I don't know where Fred is, but you can come in if you like."

The apartment was small, with a living room window big enough for a view across the river to Sarnia, Ontario. There were lighted candles on just about every table and a picture of Jesus on the wall just above one of those fake fireplaces with plastic logs. If she had a car, there'd probably be a plastic Jesus on the dashboard. The room smelled of incense and was clean and tidy. She told Angelo to have a seat and then proceeded to talk.

"You probably know all about me. The heroin habit I kicked. The two years I spent at Huron Valley Correctional in Ypsilanti. My years in prostitution, mostly the high end of Woodward Avenue, and places like the lounges at Topinka's and The Brass Rail, I'll have you know. And my years in the movies."

She lit a Lucky Strike from one of the candles, took a deep drag, her eyes still holding his.

"You know, I didn't always look like this. In my younger days I had quite the figure. Lush was how they described me."

With all the candles, the smell of incense, and that photo of Jesus looking down at him, Angelo felt like he was in a church, hearing her confession, but a confession with a bucket full of pride. He wasn't here to give her absolution he just wanted to know where the fuck he could find her husband.

"Mrs. Nowak, when was the last time you saw Fred?"

"I caught him cheating on me. Can you believe that?"

"Do you know who she was?"

"He had a box full of dirty magazines hidden under the stairs. Playboy."

This was all getting surreal. Angelo felt like telling her that maybe Fred was just looking at Playboy for the articles, but he figured she might not get the joke. Angelo was a whiz at thinking up tricks but he decided to play it straight.

"Is that why you left him?"

"Yes… and that other thing."

"What other thing?"

"Why the movies, of course."

"Movies, what movies?"

"You know, Fred wanted to get back in the business."

Angelo headed back to Detroit as fast as a six-cylinder Ford could get out of its own way. He didn't get much from Fred's old lady but it was something. He left his business card with her in case Fred tried to contact her. Angelo felt sorry for the woman, but then he wondered if it was all an act. She could be sitting there in her apartment sipping on a beer and laughing up her sleeve at him. Had she really found Jesus? The way she talked, maybe she missed the old days. Hooking up with johns. Being a blue movie star. Dreaming guys still wanted to get her in the sack. For now, Angelo decided to give her the benefit of the doubt.

Laurel Gray stood in the upstairs apartment of an old store front on Michigan Avenue just west of Livernois. She'd chucked the short shorts and now wore a black knit suit tailored to fit snugly with a satin white blouse open enough at the collar that if one were taller than the bottom of her chin, one could get a nice view of an excess amount of cleavage. Her hair was pulled back tight in a bun and black framed glasses gave her the look of a young professional. A lawyer, accountant, vice-president of a bank maybe.

She watched Fred Nowak tinker with a 16-millimeter Ariflex movie camera on a tri-pod. The room was set up to be a studio with overhead lights, reflectors, and a fancy new bed. Fred wore a pair of old work pants, an un-tucked sleeveless undershirt and black Converse All Star basketball shoes. Sweat dripped off the tip of his nose.

Laurel moved to the front of the camera.

"You look like a train wreck. Get some new clothes."

Fred wiped sweat away from his face with the palm of his hand.

"Get an air conditioner in here, I might not look so bad."

"Skip's picking one up."

She walked around him. Studying him.

"You need to look more like a director. Maybe get a black beret. Yeah, I see you all dressed in black. Like one of those Italian or French directors."

Laurel was only half-kidding. Fred hated her, wanted to say something, put the bitch in her place. She could be sweet and girly when the mood fit her but around him, she was never in that kind of mood. They were paying him twice what he made at the Anchor Bar, and the work was going to be steady, so he kept his mouth shut.

Laurel walked out into the small narrow hallway where a skinny, less than average looking man about thirty-five sat in a metal folding chair. His hair had receded halfway to the top of his head. He wore a bathrobe and his legs were hairy. Black socks and black wingtip shoes looked to be about size twelve. Laurel approached him.

"You sure you can do this?"

He looked her square in the eye.

"Piece of cake."

Laurel walked away, then looked back.

"Loose the shoes and socks, please."

Skip Ten Eyck sat behind his used Steelcase desk with a young, pretty redhead named Anna Capri in his lap. Her face was spotted with a few freckles. She had on baby doll pajamas and her feet were bare. This was one of the other upstairs apartments now converted into an office with a Persian rug on the floor and a couple of plastic potted plants. When Laurel entered Skip gave her a big smile.

"What's up, babe?"

Laurel moved behind another desk in the corner opposite his. This was her space, with a Royal typewriter, Brothers adding machine, and a vase with real flowers. When he called her babe, it rattled her nerves, but the big dumb hotshot son of a bitch was so sure of himself that he didn't even seem to care that it was she who called the shots. He took the credit, and that's what mattered to him.

Laurel stood behind her desk and watched Skip with Anna doing a little number on his lap. Two years ago, she was almost in the same place, but without the baby dolls. She had on a size too small sack dress and hadn't taken a bath in almost a week. The sweat, carnie dirt and work tan gave her a swarthy look as she sat behind that three-card-Monte table when Skip walked into the tent that she shared with the fortune teller. Laurel was a seller but wasn't a joke teller, relying on common sense and not afraid to gamble, that's why she left with him. But she never let him put her in his lap.

She looked at Skip with a calm expression.

"Can we talk? In private."

Skip gave Anna a kiss on the cheek, nudged her from his lap, then patted her bottom.

"Go get him, sweetheart; show me what you got."

After Anna left, Laurel walked to the front of Skip's desk.

"You were going to pick up another window air conditioner from Sears. When?"

"I'll do it tonight, babe."

Laurel walked over to the window and stood in front of the air conditioner and let the cool air chill her backside.

"How old is she?"

"Old enough."

Laurel double checked every girl that worked for Skip. He was cavalier about it, but it was she that needed to save his bacon if push came to shove. If he got busted, she'd go down with him. She flipped up her suit jacket and blouse and let the cold air hit her naked back.

"Stick this in the window of the other room. We wouldn't want little Miss Muffet with the freckles getting too hot and bothered."

Angelo stormed through the front door of Walt's Camera shop. The last time he was there, he played games with Walt's widow and let her get the upper hand. He wasn't going to let that happen again. She recognized him the second the bell over the door stopped ringing.

"Well, hey there, sport, got another roll of film of you and the little lady?"

Angelo slapped his police badge on the counter in front of her and gave her a cold look.

"You can keep your foot off the pedal. If I hear that Jap camera click, or the sound of a tape recorder, I'll get a search warrant and storm this joint with a fist-full of cops and violate you on a morals beef. Then let you stew in lockup for a couple of nights. Catch my drift?"

She took a deep, nonchalant breath.

"What do you want?"

"How far back do you go with Fred Nowak?"

"Fred? He used to bring his film in here all the time when my husband was alive."

"You haven't seen him since?"

"I didn't say that. Look, you can take me downtown, lock me up, search this place, you don't need a warrant. What I'm trying to say is I'm not in the business anymore."

That stumped Angelo. He thought he'd come in here and play the bad cop, now it looks like she's playing games.

"Why aren't you in the business anymore?"

"Because Fred came in here two weeks ago and bought me out."

"Fred bought the store?"

"No. He bought a used 16-millimeter Ariflex movie camera, tripods, lights and every 100-foot roll of color film I had plus all my chemicals and darkroom equipment. I had a bunch of stag films cluttering up the place so I threw those in as part of the deal. Some girl who looked young enough to be his daughter helped him load it all into a van. He paid me in cash, and off they went."

"A little blonde in a pony tail?"

"Don't they all have pony tails these days?"

Angelo turned that over.

"Let me guess, they didn't leave any forwarding address."

"You guessed right, son."

Angelo picked his badge off the counter and stuffed it in his pocket, gave her one last look, then started to walk away.

"You need film developed there's always Cunningham's."

Angelo pulled open the door. He felt like saying something, but held back. Let the old broad get in the last lick. What did it matter?

The downstairs of the abandoned storefront on Michigan Avenue was empty except for two large banquet tables. On each table were several Maxwell House coffee cans filled with fresh cut marijuana. This is how the operation worked. Skip's cousin in San Diego, the same cousin who sent him his beloved Huarache sandals, smuggled the dope across the border from Tijuana, packed it in the coffee cans, boxed them up in plain cardboard and shipped them by United Parcel Service from California to Skip in Michigan.

The girls Skip employed, when they weren't busy being party girls or making movies, could crash upstairs in two of the apartments and head downstairs to roll joints on those big long tables. One corner of the room was partitioned off with new plywood and a door that read *Darkroom*.

In another corner was a table with an old editing machine. On a table sat a Keystone 16-millimeter movie projector pointed at a large white sheet tacked to the wall. About a dozen folding metal chairs were positioned in two rows in front of the screen.

Upstairs in Skip's office, a business conference was in session. Skip sat behind his desk with his feet on it. Laurel sat on the corner of her desk with a bottle of Coke in her hand. Fred Nowak was leaned up against a wall. Anna Capri, the young redhead with the freckles and baby doll pajamas, sat on a love seat with her knees tucked up under her chin, smoking a cigarette. Fred looked over at Skip.

"You know, not just any guy can walk in off the street and do this."

Skip got up from behind his desk and walked over to Anna on the loveseat and put his hand under her chin gently cradling her face.

"Look at this. She's a walking, living wet dream."

Anna stubbed out her cigarette in an ashtray.

"I did everything I could; besides his breath was really bad."

Laurel took a swig of Coke.

"Okay, here's the situation. Our first film's a flop, no joke intended, and not because of anything any of us did. How do we get everything up on its feet? Fred, you're the expert here, what do we do?"

"Every guy I worked with years ago is either too old to get it up anymore, dead, or in jail. You're the youngsters, so I guess the ball's in your court."

That's not what Skip and Laurel wanted to hear. In the following moments of silence, the place felt empty.

TWENTY-FOUR

It was a typical gloomy November day in Detroit, a Wednesday. There hadn't been a full day of sunshine since the beginning of the month and Thanksgiving was next week. Angelo was coming off a bad couple of months. The murder case on Sylvia Coyne had gone cold with no leads. He'd been up one street and down the next and each one ended in a dead end.

The girl had no fingerprints on file and no identification that could be found. No missing persons file matched her description and no one had come forward. As for finding Fred Nowak it was if he disappeared from the face of the earth.

Angelo sat at the end of the bar in Detroit's Brass Rail on Michigan Avenue and wished for sunshine on this cloudy day. Maybe it would throw some light on this case. The Brass Rail wasn't all that classy, but the matchbook covers claimed it had the longest bar in the state of Michigan. Guess you could claim anything on a pack of matches unless someone called you on it.

And no one ever did as far as Angelo knew, but he hung out here every now and then. He liked their burgers.

Back at police headquarters, Angelo sat at his desk with Sylvia Coyne's file in front of him. The clock on the wall read 4:20 and the window wasn't letting in much light. It would be dark soon. After months chasing down leads, he'd get bits of information but nothing solid. More questions than answers. Who was her pimp? Did she work alone? Was Fred Nowak her killer? He was about to hang it up for the day when the phone rang.

TWENTY-FIVE

Cliff and Roger Brinks were identical twins. They used to deliver papers for Skip Ten Eyck. They dropped out of school in the tenth grade, were into petty theft, mostly stealing cigarette vending machines and busting them open for the coins and the smokes. They had toys for brains, most of them broken. When they turned eighteen, they got jobs at Ford's River Rouge plant in the steel division stoking coal into blast furnaces eight hours a day.

No matter what day of the year, it was always a good one-hundred and ten degrees where they worked. Working with their shirts off most of the time and all that shoveling gave them body builder muscles. When Skip Ten Eyck offered some part time night work that paid in cash, all of it under the table, they jumped at the chance. Since they were used to working topless, losing their pants wasn't a problem.

Laurel Gray sat behind her desk in the upstairs apartment on Michigan Avenue. There was a movie being made next door and Anna Capri's fake moans, groans and dirty talk were playing on her nerves. The Brinks brothers unscripted dialog was heavy on yeah, oh yeah, and that's it. Why bother, she kept asking herself, they were making silent stag films, so who cared?

Laurel couldn't stand the Brinks brothers. They gave her the willies. She paid them from the cash in the safe, but they liked to linger around too long after wearing out their welcome. They earned half of what the girls made and that was par for the business. They didn't seem to mind. Liked to joke that they were stokers during the day and strokers at night. They'd laugh themselves silly over that, but what really got under Laurel's skin was they kept kidding her about why she didn't get in on the action.

Skip was the man behind the camera tonight playing director. Fred took the night off. But Laurel had said goodbye to that part of the business back in August. Skip ran the show. She still kept the books on everything and booked girls for frat, stag, and bachelor parties. The reefer business downstairs was a gold mine, but the overhead on the movie business was killing them. She lobbied to axe the thing, but Skip wanted to give it more time. They argued about it, but she never got anywhere.

She was working on a long-range plan, but Skip couldn't see ten minutes in front of him. Her plan was coming together tonight. Laurel was ready to pull an ace out of her sleeve and it involved those books she kept and the numbers she crunched and a suitcase under her desk.

The Brinks brothers strolled into Laurel's office after working up a good sweat double-teaming Anna Capri in the room next door. Laurel could smell them as soon as they got six feet from her desk.

"There's a shower down the hall. Why don't you ever use it?"

Cliff Brinks ran his fingers through his wet, jet black hair, trying to comb it and keep it out of his eyes. He grinned at Laurel.

"This is love sweat, sweetheart, that animal scent that makes women hot to trot."

"Sweat is sweat and the two of you smell like dogs left out in the rain too long."

Roger Brinks chuckled at that dig.

"What kind of dogs? Big dogs? Hey, did you hear about the little shit who went to Alaska and came back a Husky fucker?"

The Brinks brothers had a good laugh over that stupid joke at Laurel's expense. Disgusted, she stood up, walked to the safe, bent down and spun the combination dial. Cliff tried another joke.

"Since you don't like us very much, maybe you could just give us the combination and that would save you the time and trouble."

The brothers giggled like a couple of hyenas.

Laurel took out some cash, closed the safe, stood, and placed it on her desk, then took a couple of steps back.

"There you go, a day's pay for a couple hours of work."

Cliff and Roger scooped up the money and stuffed it into their pockets. Roger flashed a slick grin.

"How come we don't get no overtime?"

"What, you think this is a union shop? Now get the hell out of my office."

They backed up toward the door grinning like two Cheshire cats. Roger gave her a little wink.

"Little touchy tonight, ain't ya?"

Laurel's eyes like ice as she slammed the door in their faces.

TWENTY-SIX

Angelo headed north on I-94 for Port Huron. That phone call was from Carla Nowak, Fred's wife. Said she had some news on Fred. She couldn't tell him over the phone, wanted to tell him in person and could he drive up to see her. He pumped her for information but she insisted she had to see him. It began to rain when Angelo got out of his car and headed up to her apartment.

When she answered the door this time, things looked different. Carla had washed and set her hair, had make-up on that took a few years off, and wore a tight dress that clung to her skinny frame. She wobbled some when she spoke.

"Please come in."

Inside the apartment, the picture of Jesus was missing in action, and there were only two candles lit on the coffee table in front of the sofa. Two bottles of cheap wine were on the table with two glasses. One of the bottles had already been drained, the other recently uncapped. It didn't take a brain surgeon to figure something was up. He wondered if he was wrong about Carla the first time he was here, and had given her the benefit of the doubt. She purred with a slur.

"Can I get you something?"

Angelo didn't like the tone of that purr. The woman was wet-eyed drunk.

"I'm here, so what's up with Fred?"

Carla slithered over to the couch and sat, pulling a fluffy cushion behind her back and crossing her legs.

"Get comfortable. Pour yourself a drink."

Angelo didn't want any part of this con from a sad, lonely woman. He checked his watch.

"Look, Mrs. Nowak, it's almost seven. It's dark and it's raining, and I've got a long drive back to Detroit. If you've seen or talked to Fred, I'd appreciate if you'd tell me right now."

She kept mum and poured herself a glass of wine, smiled, got up and walked to the bedroom door then disappeared into the room. Angelo wanted to leave, but he was going to get some answers from her come hell or high water.

"Mrs. Nowak, we can either talk here or you can hitch a ride with me to police headquarters in Detroit."

There was a moment of silence before he could hear her crying in the bedroom.

"Shit."

He walked to the bedroom door and looked in. Carla was reclined on the bed with her head up against a couple of big pillows. The room was dark except for one end table light next to her on the bed. Angelo walked toward her.

And that's when he saw it. There was a college textbook lying on the end table. The title in gold letters, *Human Anatomy*, illuminated by the warm glow of the lamp. Angelo felt a sharp pain in the back of his head, and that's when the lights went out.

A Greyhound bus headed north on I-75. The flip sign above the windshield read Sault Ste. Marie, Ontario. A hard rain was falling and the wipers were having a hard time keeping up. Inside, there were about twenty passengers scattered about. Laurel Gray sat alone with a row all to herself. She wore the black suit she liked, the one that gave her the look of a professional young woman, and a tan London Fog trench coat. It would be early morning Thursday before she arrived in Ontario, and late Friday before she made it to Saskatchewan.

She'd left her office after Skip had cleared out. Two of Skip's girls were sound asleep in one of the other apartments. The two company books were stacked neatly on her desk and fresh flowers were in the vase next to the typewriter. The combination safe in the corner was locked. It's how she left the office every day.

Laurel stared out the bus window at the open countryside, what little she could see of it, and ran over in her mind all the parts of her plan. Leave with no trace. All the clothes and jewelry Skip bought her still hung in the closet or were stuffed away in a drawer. The suitcase on the seat next to her was filled with twenty-five thousand dollars in cash, money she managed to skim the past two years. No one would be the wiser. Not even Skip. The books were in order and there was over a hundred grand still locked in the safe.

Laurel opened her purse and took out a small stuffed bear. She knew her daughter wouldn't know her. She hadn't had any contact with her or her mother in almost five years. She thought about buying a bunch of expensive toys, but nixed that idea, didn't want to overwhelm the little girl. Skimming the money from Skip, cooking the books, that was easy. Being a mom to a little girl who would look at her as a stranger could be a kick in the gut. Laurel had a lot of work to do and holding that bear in her hands gave her a glimmer of hope.

John Angelo woke up in Carla Nowak's living room with a splitting headache. The first image he saw after the fog cleared from his eyes was the barrel of his own gun about three inches from his nose. Fred Nowak held the gun. He wore leather driving gloves and his face cracked a half-smirk of a smile.

"Welcome back to the real world. Did you have nice dreams?"

Angelo tried to move, but he was seated in an upright kitchen chair with his arms over the back and his wrists laced with his own handcuffs.

He saw Carla on the sofa. Most of that second bottle of wine was gone and she was three sheets to the wind.

Angelo blinked his eyes and tried to clear the cobwebs.

"I dreamed that I drove all the way out here and this asshole of a murderer would be hiding under the bed."

Fred pushed the barrel of the gun into the tip of Angelo's nose.

"Should've looked behind the door, dipshit."

"I killed the bitch. The fucking whore."

Those slurred words came from Carla. Was this half-ass Jesus freak covering for her old man? Angelo put a hard stare on Fred.

"You are a real piece of work."

Fred jammed the barrel of the gun under Angelo's chin.

"No, it's true. My wife here is the jealous type. She did find Jesus, or so she says, and she did kick me out, but I couldn't let her go down for this, so I dumped the girl's body in the fountain on Belle Isle. Made it look like just another whore done in by some angry john. You were getting too close for comfort, so I had to come up with another plan. Here's the scoop: I drive you back to Detroit in your car and we motor out to Belle Isle, park by the fountain. I stick you behind the wheel, put the barrel of your gun in your mouth and pull the trigger. Sylvia Coyne's college book is on the seat next to you, along with her purse and ID. Your detective buddies figure it all out. Rogue cop, full of guilt does himself in. All wrapped up like a Christmas present. Don't even need no bow."

Angelo turned that over and wiggled around in the chair.

"How are you going to get off Belle Isle? You going to walk?"

"Carla follows in my car."

Angelo looked over at Carla, still sipping on that glass of wine.

"Yeah? You must have shit for brains. She's got two bottles of wine in her. How much you want to bet she gets pulled over on a DUI by the State Cops before she's a mile outside Port Huron?"

Fred had a look on his face that said maybe he should have thought this out better.

"She'll sober up."

"Take a look at her, Fred. I'd say she's going to pass out and sleep it off. Probably won't wake up until morning."

Fred's eyes glinted, the anger boiling up.

"Shut the fuck up."

Angelo piled it on.

"Carla called me at work. There'll be a record of that. Oh, and there's going to be a goose egg the size of a golf ball on the back of my head. Did you think of that? Those forensics boys are no dummies. Yeah, it's a Christmas present. But you'll need a bow on it, a really big one. Only problem, the box is empty."

Fred's heard enough.

"Stand up."

Angelo stood, and with his right hand gripped to the chair, brought it up with him. Before Fred could react or say anything, Angelo spun around and caught Fred under the chin with one leg of the chair. It knocked him back into the wall as Angelo thrust the legs of the chair into Fred and pinned him against the wall. Fred tried to bring the gun up to Angelo's head, but Angelo was too quick. He spun around again and kicked Fred hard in the balls. Fred collapsed against the wall then slumped to the floor. Angelo kicked the gun out of his hand and finished him off with another blow to the head. Carla jumped up.

"You leave my husband alone."

She dropped the wine glass, then passed out, her limp body crashing across the coffee table.

The clock on the wall in the interrogation room back at Detroit police headquarters read midnight. Fred Nowak sat at a table. Across from him sat Angelo. Angelo put a Chesterfield between Fred's lips and lit it. Captain O'Dowd stood over in the corner. Fred took a deep drag on the cigarette.

"My wife, she gonna be okay?"

Angelo lit a Chesterfield for himself, offered one to O'Dowd who shook his head no.

"How long you known me, Fred?"

"I don't know, ten years maybe?"

"Have I always been a straight shooter?"

"Yeah, I got no complaints, other than you kicking the shit out of me."

Angelo took a drag on his cigarette.

"Carla's over in the emergency room at Henry Ford. They're pumping her stomach. They found a bottle of sleeping pills in her purse, most of them gone. Did you know she took those before she started chugging two bottles of cheap wine?"

Fred now feeling guilt, sensing where this might be going.

"No. Are you gonna give it to me straight?"

"There's a fifty-fifty chance she'll make it, Fred."

Fred hung his head and started to cry.

Angelo continued, but softened his tone, not trying to poke him.

"Were you pimping the girl, Sylvia Coyne?"

"No. I was just tryin' to help her out."

"You're fifty years old, Fred. What was the plan for helping out a girl barely out of her bobby sox? Were you fucking her?"

Fred wasn't shut-my-mouth shocked at that. He sat up ramrod straight in his chair.

"Why not. She was workin' the streets solo, mostly in Corktown, sometimes out on Warren on the west side. She took the bus a lot. I told her about this guy I met, might have a better, safer deal for her, called himself Paper Boy. He was runnin' girls her age for parties, stuff like that. I was shooting stag films for him."

"Was she with you when you bought all that photography stuff from Walt Robbins' widow?"

"Yeah, she said she thought she'd be good doin' movies like that. She liked the idea that they'd be in color."

Angelo looked over at O'Dowd. He was probably thinking the same thing as Angelo. And what Angelo was thinking was that if Fred really wanted to help this girl, he'd have driven her home to her parents, if she had any, or dropped her off at the St.

Francis D'Assisi convent over on Buchanan. Angelo held back his anger.

"This paper boy, does he have a name?"

"Skip Ten Eyck. He set up shop over on Michigan Avenue, just west of Livernois. Some of the girls live upstairs. That's where we shoot the movies. Main floor is used for his drug stuff and my darkroom."

"What kind of drug stuff?"

"Reefers, some amyl nitrate poppers but no hard stuff."

"This paper boy living there too?"

"Don't know where he lives, but he's there most of the time. Drives one of those fancy new Corvette convertibles.

TWENTY-SEVEN

It was eight o'clock in the morning on the Friday before Thanksgiving and Skip Ten Eyck's Corvette was parked on the main floor of the abandoned building on Michigan Avenue. There were cops everywhere you could spit loading up boxes of Maxwell House Coffee cans into a police van. Too many boxes to count. Skip, the Paper Boy, was busted soon as he drove into the place and was hauled away in cuffs.

There were two girls upstairs who'd managed to sleep through the initial police raid, but woke up when they heard all the racket downstairs. The girls were given a choice. Go home or go to the convent. They chose to go home after they were booked and photographed downtown.

Angelo stood in the darkroom and looked through a cardboard box filled with metal movie cans, each labeled with a title and date. Many of them were dated from the 1940's and 1950's. Walt's widow told him that Fred bought out all her old stock and there were some nasty titles. No home movies of the kids at Christmas or Junior's birthday party or anything like that.

One film grabbed Angelo's attention. It was dated 1962. There was no title. He opened up the can and took out the roll of eight-millimeter film. He pulled about two feet of film from the reel and held it up to the light. It was color film, and that's when he recognized the small image of a woman. Didn't need to screen it on any movie projector. Wasn't going to douse the lights and show the boys in the next room the high-octane babe getting her game on. He knew he had one more thing to do before he could wrap up this whole nightmare. The one that began almost a year ago on a cold Detroit night in the month of December, 1962, just before a Christmas that would never be merry.

TWENTY-EIGHT

Laurel Gray got off the bus in Sault St. Marie, Ontario and had a two-hour layover before the next bus to Regina, Saskatchewan. The bus station in Sault St. Marie was small and only offered soda pop and candy bar vending machines.

It was eight in the morning and she couldn't even remember the last time she'd had a good meal. There was a small diner across the street that was open, and a breakfast of eggs, bacon, toast, and endless cups of coffee sounded like just the ticket on a bitter November day where six inches of snow already blanketed the ground.

Laurel's suitcase was heavy, and she spotted a rack of coin operated storage lockers next to the Coke machine. There were twelve lockers, three rows of four. The bottom two rows were occupied so she dropped a quarter in locker number eleven on the top row. She turned the key and popped open the door, and started to lift the suitcase to the locker. Even though she was a long limbed five feet eight inches tall, it was a stretch and the weight was hard to handle. She heard a man's voice behind her.

"Here let met help you with that."

An elderly man about eighty who looked like Santa Claus helped her stash the suitcase in the locker. He closed the door, locked it, and gave Laurel the key. She said thanks and was about to walk away.

"Where are you traveling to?"

Laurel's stomach was grumbling and she was anxious to get to that diner across the street and wasn't in the mood for chit chat or small talk, but her Canadian prairie upbringing taught her not to be rude to elders. About the only value she managed to cling to in her young adult life.

"I'm going to Saskatchewan."

The old man had a twinkle in his eye.

"The heartland, amber waves of grain, but only wind-swept landscapes of bitter cold and snow this time of the year."

Laurel smiled, but couldn't think of anything to say.

"Are you visiting friends out there?"

"Family."

"The wife and I are headed for Toronto."

He nodded to a gray-haired woman about his age seated in the waiting area.

"Got a new granddaughter we're going to visit. That makes six altogether."

"How wonderful."

"The wife and I were going to get some breakfast across the street. Would you like to join us?"

Laurel turned that over. Nice old couple. Probably about the same age as the grandparents she never knew. They never made it over from Ukraine.

"Don't mind if I do."

She put the locker key in her pocket and walked across the street with the old couple.

Laurel ordered the Big Breakfast. Eggs, hash browns, bacon and all the pancakes you could stick on a plate. She knew she couldn't eat everything but the smell of the place made her even hungrier and it sure looked yummy when the waitress set that large plate on the counter in front of her.

She ate like a horse, between sips of black coffee. The elderly couple ordered just coffee and Danish. The woman proudly showed Laurel photos of her grandkids. Her husband talked about his hardware store and how business was kind of slow this time of year. They asked Laurel if she was a lawyer or banker since she was dressed so nice.

Laurel made up a story, laid it on as thick as the Karo syrup that smothered her pancakes. Said she sold real estate near Detroit and was headed home to Saskatchewan for a family visit.

The couple finished their coffee and Danish and then left, headed back to the bus station. As Laurel finished her breakfast, she tried to think about what she would say to her mom when she got back home, but words weren't coming easy. She'd have to get some kind of job. Put that twenty-five grand into a bank account or stocks or bonds. That would be the nest egg for her daughter.

And then it hit her like a sledge hammer. She left so fast all those years ago that she never even gave the little girl a name. Tears filled her eyes, so she wiped them away with her napkin. Maybe her mom gave the baby away. Or she kept her, and wouldn't give up the baby to Laurel. All this took her appetite away. She took one last sip of coffee and left five bucks on the counter.

Back in the bus terminal, Laurel walked to the storage lockers, removed the key from her pocket and saw that there already was a key in locker eleven. She looked at the number on her key. It read twelve.

"Shit".

There were a few people in the terminal that heard, but didn't give it much attention.

She opened locker twelve, it was empty. She dropped a quarter into locker eleven. Empty. Laurel wanted to scream, kick the shit out of the metal, pound on the lockers with her fists. She fell for the oldest con in the books. The old guy palmed the key for number eleven, while he slipped her the key to number twelve. All that time running the three-card-monte game, working for Skip and skimming all that cash without him having a clue, and an old guy with a sweet face and friendly voice scammed her out of the rest of her life.

Laurel composed herself and walked over to the ticket window and confronted the agent.

"There was an old couple in here about an hour ago going to Toronto, what time did that bus leave?"

"The bus for Toronto doesn't leave until one o'clock this afternoon."

That hit Laurel like a hard fist to the face.

"An old couple, gray hair, the guy had a face looked like Santa Claus, they were sitting right over there. I had breakfast with them. Did you see them leave?"

"Yeah, but not on a bus, a young guy came in and picked them up."

Laurel wanted to tear her hair out, reach across the counter and even tear the ticket agent's hair out. She tried to think, but her anger messed up her brain. She thought about calling the police, but the old farts were probably long gone. Besides, if the cops or Mounties tracked them down, how would she explain all that money? She put herself together, took a few deep breaths and said to the ticket agent.

"The bus that came in from Detroit this morning, when does it return to Detroit?"

"Leaves in about fifteen minutes."

Laurel gave that a couple of seconds.

"Give me a ticket."

She paid the agent thirteen dollars and fifty-five cents for the one-way to Detroit and had a seat in the waiting area. All she could do for the next five minutes was stare out the window, making plans for what she would do once she got back to Detroit.

What would she say? It took her two years to skim twenty-five thousand bucks. Maybe she could just grab the hundred-grand from the safe and beat feet again. Nothing she thought of was making any sense.

A young mother with her little girl came into the terminal and sat in the seats opposite Laurel. The girl looked to be about six years old. She began making a fuss, giving her mom a difficult time and wouldn't settle down. Laurel reached in her purse and pulled out that stuffed bear she bought and gave it to the little girl. The child smiled. And it put her at peace.

The mom said, "You didn't have to do that."

"I think she needs it more than I do."

"Thank you, you have a kind heart."

Laurel sat there and watched the child play with the stuffed bear for the next five minutes. And in that time the anger that was churning inside her, so evident on her face moments ago when she opened those empty lockers, was gone. She thought of her own daughter now. She'd be as sweet as this little girl. She'd love the mother she never knew. Over the public address, the ticket agent spoke.

"Greyhound bus 668 for Detroit now boarding."

Laurel looked at the ticket for Detroit in her hand, and then looked at the little girl sitting there with a smile on her face playing with that bear. Laurel got up, walked to a trash can, tore the Detroit ticket in half and tossed it.

She walked back to her seat and sat down. Laurel closed her eyes and tried to think pleasant thoughts. Her daughter would be close to six years old now. About the same age as the little girl playing with that stuffed bear in the seat across from her. Her daughter would be a happy, well-adjusted child, eager to finally see her mother. She wouldn't be angry. She'd understand why her mother left her. She'd forgive. They'd hug, and cry, and the past would be forgotten.

A couple of minutes into those thoughts, the little girl started to act up again. The stuffed bear seemed to have lost its magic. Laurel opened her eyes and watched as the little girl tossed the bear at her. It sailed over Laurel's head and landed on the dirty concrete floor. Laurel shot the little girl a half-curious and half-hostile stare. The mom was embarrassed.

"I'm sorry. The terrible twos are going on six."

Laurel thought about getting up and giving the bear back to the little girl, but then the child stuck her tongue out at her. Laurel stuck her tongue out at the little girl. The mom grabbed her daughter, wrapped her in her arms, and stood up.

"That's very rude and no way to treat a child."

The mom and her kid stormed away and headed for the candy vending machine.

Laurel sat there a moment. The anger was back. She thought about the money in the suitcase, all the crap she had to put up with to get it, only to have it conned from her by Mr. and Mrs. Santa Claus. She'd get back to Moose Jaw the same way she left. Flat broke with only the clothes on her back. She heard the ticket agent on the PA.

"Final boarding for bus 668 to Detroit."

Laurel stood and walked behind her and picked up the stuffed bear from the floor. She brushed the dirt off the fur, walked to the trash can and pulled out the torn ticket to Detroit. Then she jammed the stuffed bear into the trash.

TWENTY-NINE

John Angelo was half-way through the Detroit-Windsor tunnel. Even with the windows rolled up, one could still smell the exhaust fumes. They never went away, locked in this two-way traffic tomb of dim light and dirty white subway tile. The radio played nothing but static.

When Angelo exited on the Canadian side, he rolled his window down, killed the volume on the radio and showed the border officer his police badge. He got waved through without a hitch.

He cranked the radio up and made his way through downtown Windsor to Wyandotte street. A local DJ was spinning a song by some British pop band he'd never heard of. "I wanna hold hands," or something like that. Teeny-bopper crap. He shut it off.

On Wyandotte Street he parked in front of a bar called The Tiger Tail Lounge. You couldn't miss the large red neon sign and blinking lights that screamed *GIRLS, GIRLS, GIRLS.*

A sign in the window read *Open at Noon, Now Serving Businessmen's Lunch.*

He walked into a bar that looked like your average neighborhood joint with tables and chairs and the smell of liquor and fried food. But there were bar girls in skimpy tiger-striped baby-doll pajamas and high heels serving drinks to middle-aged men dressed in business suits, and a nearly naked young girl dancing on a table in the center of the room.

She looked to be about seventeen under all that heavy makeup, or maybe it was Clearasil. Either way, she was a looker. She had long coal black hair and her dark skin looked to be the result of heritage. She wore a skimpy buckskin bikini with strands of leather fringe. On her head was a headband with a feather and in her hand was a wooden tomahawk. She danced around like at an Indian Pow Wow, stomping her feet to the beat of the song *Running Bear* that played on the smooth sounding stereo hi-fi.

Angelo remembered the song from a few years back. One of the vice-cops he worked with was half Huron Indian and took offense at the nature and lyrics to the song. Angelo didn't think much about it at the time, but then the more he thought about it, he could see the guy's point. Indians always seemed to be catching the short end of the stick from the white man.

Angelo hoped to catch Velma Turnbull here. If not, maybe they'd give him the address to the apartment where she shacked up with her divorce lawyer. He'd lost it. He didn't need an address. As soon as he sat at the bar, he recognized Velma. She was serving up drinks like a pro, popping the tops off bottles of beer and passing bottles of gin and whiskey from hand to hand in an orchestrated ballet.

Velma spotted Angelo out of the corner of her eye and came over. She looked good, no worse for wear, dressed all in black. She gave Angelo a sultry wink.

"Hey, champ, long time no see."

Angelo matched her wink.

"You got a few minutes to talk?"

She waved at the other bartender, a woman about the same age as Velma.

"Cover for me, will you, Suzie?"

Velma stepped out from behind the bar and walked Angelo over to an empty table in a corner away from all the action and sat down across from him.

"Kind of out of your jurisdiction for a Detroit vice cop, aren't you?"

Angelo flashed her a cheap smile.

"Got anything good to eat in here?"

"Not really. The Clam Shack over on Chatham has a good seafood lunch buffet."

Angelo turned around, took a gaze at the stripper dancing on the table and peeling off that bikini.

"Princess Summer-Fall-Winter-Spring chase you off the stage, put you behind the bar?"

Velma had a laugh at that.

"That's funny. But here's a real kicker. Did you know that the actress who played Princess Summer-Fall-Winter-Spring on the *Howdy Doody Show* put out for Buffalo Bob and the crew?"

Angelo looked a little skeptical.

"That a fact."

"She quit the show after a couple of years, played Elvis Presley's girlfriend in *Jailhouse Rock* and two days after filming ended, she was killed in a head on car crash."

"You're making all this up."

"No. It's true. One day someone will probably write a book about it. You'd be surprised all the useless crap you learn tending bar."

Velma directed Angelo's attention back to the girl on stage.

"Her name's Yvette, nineteen years old from the sticks in Quebec. She's full-blooded Algonquin and get this, she doesn't speak a lick of English. Works the noon till eight shift six days a week. Calls herself Little White Dove. Just like in the song. You know, little White Dove lived on the other side of the river from Running Bear. Their tribes were at war. They were in love. They dove into the river to be together and the raging river pulled them down. Guess they'll always be together in that happy hunting ground. Corny, isn't it? But on a good day she'll walk out of here with two hundred in tips, mostly fives and tens, and most of it American. And the girl's a sweetheart, a real straight arrow, no disrespect. Doesn't fool around. Her boyfriend works the line at the Ford engine plant here in Windsor and is built like a mountain."

Angelo gave Velma a long look.

"Are you telling me it's hard to compete? I've seen you dance. What gives? You've still got the body and the moves. What happened to the Marilyn Monroe routine?"

Velma shot him a warm smile that said thank you behind her heavy red lipstick.

"Moves don't cut it any more, honey. The guys that come in here don't want to pay to look at a woman same age as their wife, they pay to look at someone the same age as their daughter."

He didn't know why, but Angelo felt like reaching across the table and taking hold of her hand.

"Are you doing okay?"

"If you're asking about my attorney friend, well he got tired of looking at me about the same time I started schlepping drinks. Course when his wife got wind of the setup that was the final nail in the coffin. I found a little studio apartment a couple of blocks away. It's nice to be able to walk to work. Plus, just about all my tips are American.

There was a long pause. What could Angelo say? I'm so sorry, told you so.

"You didn't come all the way over here to check on my sex life, did you?"

Velma gave him a faint provocative smile, the same look she'd give him before they always ended up jumping in the sack.

"But it would be nice to think that was the case."

Angelo reached in his pocket and took out the metal canister with the eight-millimeter film and laid it on the table in front of her. Velma looked at the label.

"1962. Wasn't such a great year, was it? This is it?"

"Yeah."

"Did you watch it?"

"Peeked at a couple of frames with a magnifier."

Velma opened the canister, pulled out the reel and held a couple of feet of film up to the lone light hanging over the table.

"This the original?"

"I think so, but there can't be that many copies. Photo lab guy at headquarters told me film gets worn and breaks, and since it's color will eventually fade and the images will disappear."

Velma smiled and put the film back in the canister and stuck it in her apron.

"Know what's funny? Last year this meant life or death to me. Now, I don't really care. Ever find those black and white negatives of me and the colored boys?"

"No. And they didn't have anything to do with that blackmail scheme. It was all on Sophia Martino."

Velma hesitated a moment.

"Figured as much."

She got up, put a hand on Angelo's shoulder. There was a sudden gleam in her eye.

"You want to hang out at my apartment? I'm done at eight and I'm off most of the day tomorrow."

"I have to work tonight. Give me a rain check?"

Velma kissed him on the cheek, smiled, then walked back to the bar.

Angelo took the Ambassador Bridge back to Detroit. The tunnel was closer and quicker, but the view from the bridge was pretty spectacular. The sunshine was hazy, but about the best you could expect this late in November. A couple of ore boats made their way downriver, headed for the steel mills and Lake Erie. He thought about Velma and her offer. He could've called in sick, and spent the night. He wondered why he seemed to always be attracted to that kind of woman. Prostitutes, stripers, damaged goods on the down slope of life.

There was that pretty blonde bank teller with creamy complexion about his age that was always so nice to him when he cashed his paycheck at Superior Trust Bank on Woodward. She didn't have a ring on her left hand. He noticed that right away. He thought about asking her out, but never did. Maybe it was the danger he sought. The risk of everything coming apart living on the edge. And how dangerous could it be with a bank teller who looked like Doris Day wearing a blouse buttoned up to her chin and smelling of White Shoulders perfume?

Tomorrow was Saturday and for a change he had the day off. Michigan was playing Ohio State in Ann Arbor. Maybe drive out there, scam a ticket off a scalper real cheap when he showed his badge. Or just sleep. Anything to relax, take his mind off the shit storm of his life.

Retirement was less than two years down the road. He could almost taste it. Think happy thoughts of Florida and endless sunshine and days on the beach. Hell, maybe even watch one of those George Perot travelogues on Sunday that Sophia loved. He'd make it a weekend to relax and put the reality of life on hold.

Angelo flicked on the radio to a Detroit station that played jazz. Chet Baker was singing *I've Never Been in Love Before.* The smooth sound of his voice coupled with the soulful sounds of his trumpet solos could make all the troubles of the world go away. Chet playing, and that glimmer of sun off the tranquil river, brought a smile to Angelo's face. And just like that, Chet stopped playing and a somber man's voice came over the radio. Angelo almost didn't hear it at first. Something about the President being shot in Dallas.

THIRTY

"The biggest beef I got in here is the heat. I mean, holy fuck, it must be a hundred degrees, and that's with that fucking window open."

Skip Ten Eyck was seated at a table in a decrepit conference room at the Ionia Correctional Facility about 40 miles northwest of Lansing, Michigan. He was right about the heat. It was late August, 1964 and Skip's prison jumpsuit was soaked in sweat.

Sitting across from Skip was John Angelo. Skip's been a regular chatterbox, bending Angelo's ear about this, that, and nothing for the past fifteen minutes. Angelo's been patient listening to Skip harangue him, rolling his finger tips on the table in a slow steady beat, wiping the sweat from his forehead with the sleeve of his white dress shirt. Skip wasn't done babbling.

"Well, I take that back. I got another burr up my ass. The food in here sucks. They slop this shit on a metal tray. Those instant mashed potatoes out of a cardboard box. Ya gotta eat them with a spoon. Know what I'm saying? Look, I know why you drove all the way up here. You and all your cop buddies are still pissed that I copped a plea with the Feds. Yeah, I rolled on my cousin in San Diego and they busted up his whole pot operation, but I'm serving two to five, and since I'm such a model prisoner, when they slop those shitty potatoes on that tray I just smile and say, 'thank you sir'. I'll be out of here in another six months. And cruising Woodward in my sixty-two Vette. So, you can just sit there and watch me sweat and I'll watch you sweat. That what you want?"

Angelo tapped his fingers one more time on the table.

"What I want first is for you to take your mouth out of first gear, and let it idle in neutral for a while. Those accounting books on your bookkeeper's desk said there was one-hundred grand in the kitty. And lo and behold we couldn't find any of it. And your dope-peddling business partner, the bookkeeper, Miss Laurel Gray is still nowhere to be found. Probably blew town. You said nothing about her and that money gone missing back when you got busted. Maybe I drove all the way up here thinking that you might be singing a different tune now that the hot weather's been doing a number on you."

Skip sat back; a shady leer twitched at the corner of his mouth.

"When you trashed my place on Michigan Avenue, stole my weed, harassed my girls, took the books, did you lift up the carpet and count the thousand-dollar bills under it?"

Skip's hunkered down, but Angelo kept digging.

"This Laurel Gray, she your main squeeze? I bet you and her cooked up this elegant little scam. She's sitting on the money somewhere waiting for her lover boy. But try this on for size. Maybe you're not her only lover boy. She could be on one of those nude beaches somewhere down south of the border sucking on limes and drinking tequila while some Mexican cabana boy slathers tanning oil all over her no tan lines body, top-to-bottom."

Skip slumped in his chair, giving Angelo a cold glare.

"Figure it out, Skip. Don't mean to pile-drive your ego, but you're not the only game in town."

Skip's face was dripping sweat.

"No, you figure it out. You're the fucking wizard. Besides, ain't you gettin' too old for this cops and robbers hanky-panky? Maybe your motor's running down, Slick."

Angelo didn't give him as much as a blink.

"Jokers like you keep me tuned up."

Angelo's had enough of Skip's hooey and shifty as smoke attitude. He stood, pushed his chair back and rolled his finger-tips one last time on the table.

"The real reason I drove up here is I wanted to know if you were smart enough to be worth talking to. Guess I wasted my time."

And with that Angelo headed for the door then turned back to Skip.

"Try soaking your bed sheets in cold water before you tuck yourself in at night. Oh, and the runny mashed potatoes?

I heard a nasty rumor that the guards spit in them. Pleasant dreams, Skipper."

As Angelo closed the door behind him, Skip sat there slack-jawed, an absent stare in his watery eyes.

Angelo headed back to Detroit on I-96. It was just after four in the afternoon, and the sun was behind him, the hot rays slanting in through the passenger side windows heating up the car. He pushed open the side window vent so the air blew directly on his face. It wasn't air conditioning, but it was enough. He was working days now. Ditched the graveyard shift three months ago and was back working Vice now as a special investigator. Not only did it give him a bump in pay, but it made an honest man out of him. No more money on the side from the payoffs for looking the other way.

He'd been trying to track down this Laurel Gray. Skip was clammed up and the girls who worked for him could only give a description of her looks. There was no record of a birth certificate in the state of Michigan or that she ever applied for a license to drive. He even had the F.B.I. run her fingerprints they pulled off the books she kept, but that came back negative.

She was smart enough to realize the heat was on. Maybe the books were cooked and she skipped town with a wad of cash. Maybe Skip had money stashed someplace. But those questions were for another day. Angelo just hoped he'd make it to Detroit by six o'clock, just in time to meet his date for dinner at Topinka's restaurant.

THIRTY-ONE

The penthouse suite at Detroit's Embassy Hotel on Washington Boulevard was tacky but lush with blood red carpet so thick you might need waders. And floor to ceiling white satin drapes. With two separate bedrooms, that left a large area filled with two over-stuffed leather sofas, a couple of wing back chairs and a few pieces of blonde mahogany furniture. It was the post-modern late 1940's, early 1950's style décor so desperately in need of an upgrade now that it was the swinging 60's. But that was probably never going to happen, what with the ups and downs of the auto industry.

Ever since General Motors moved most of its operations out of the GM Building to the Tech Center in Warren, business at the Embassy was on the down slide. High class call girls and their clients still booked rooms there and the bar was usually busy. But the Embassy, like many other Detroit establishments, was on its last legs. There was even a rumor that Hudson's Department Store would be closing up shop downtown.

A pretty young woman, bottle blonde hair with a slight wave in it circled between two poker tables set up in the middle of the room. She wore a scarlet dress that fit very tight around the hips, waist, and her ample bust. Her name was Rita Bain, a.k.a. Laurel Gray. In November of last year when Laurel caught that bus from Sault Ste. Marie back to Detroit, she knew she had to have a plan.

When the bus stopped in Saginaw for a rest stop, Laurel jumped off and spent a couple of days working on that plan. She had her hair styled and dyed blonde. She got a phony new driver's license and Social Security card that cost her fifty bucks, with a new name, Rita Bain, another Gloria Grahame character from a TV series. With her wavy blonde hair, and that sexy little permanent pout on her lips, she could have been Gloria's sister, or in a pinch, at least a second cousin. Rita scoped the room.

"Ladies, this is going to be a very special night."

The ladies Rita was talking to were five in number. Three attractive young women, maybe twenty-one, or twenty-two years in age. Two blondes and a redhead. All wore tight fitting slacks, scarlet in color that matched Rita's dress, black patent leather spiked heels and bright white blouses. Seated at those poker tables were two middle-aged women. They wore black slacks, black blouses, and black bow ties. Poker chip carousels and several thick glass ash trays decorated each table. The two women shuffled cards with the precision of pros as they sat there sober eyed listening to Rita. The room was as swanky as you could make it and Rita wasn't here to peddle Mary Jane.

One of the young blondes with hair like straw, a long neck and tired eyes stood behind a bar stacked with a boatload of booze and a couple of dozen glasses, piped up.

"What about tips? Can we keep all of it?"

Rita strolled over to her.

"Be my guest. Whatever you can squeeze out of these high-rollers, consider it well earned. They like to be flattered, especially by attractive young women. Most of these guys are in their late forties, early fifties, out of shape and overweight. They're bankers, lawyers, CEO's. Maybe even a judge or congressman thrown into the mix.

They live in the Pointes, Indian Village, Bloomfield Hills. They have money to burn, so they came downtown to the Embassy Hotel tonight for some stud poker, two-dollar beers, and four-dollar mixed drinks. Smile, lay whatever you have on thick, and if they stuff a ten or twenty down your blouse, girl you earned it."

The two middle-aged women had a hard edge to them. And it wasn't a reach to sense the resentment they felt. It was plastered on their faces. They were here to deal cards and that's all. They'd get tipped, maybe a ten spot at the end of the night. But none of these high-rollers would stuff any money down their blouses, and if they tried, they'd get a stiff hand across the face.

The other young blonde with sultry eyes chimed in.

"What if they get fresh, or out of line?"

"Let me handle that. Whatever they do, let them down easy. We don't want any conflict and no hard feelings."

The straw blonde behind the bar arranging the bottles of booze in a perfect line, poured herself a ginger ale.

"What if someone asks to meet up later someplace, what should we say?"

"The most important rule is you don't solicit. If I wanted hookers, I would have hired hookers. Now if you take a fancy to someone and he invites you somewhere for a drink and you decide to get naked with him, well, remember, you left of your own free will."

One of the other girls, a redhead named Donna, who has stayed silent, leaned against the bar, cocking her hip.

"If I fuck some guy's balls off, give him the ride of his life, and he leaves me a couple of hundred bucks, does that make me a hooker?"

That brought a laugh from the young women. The middle-aged dealers played it stoic.

Rita smiled, walked over to Donna, adjusted Donna's collar, and unbuttoned the top two buttons.

"No, I'd say that makes you one hell of a lay."

The women all had a good laugh. There was big money to made here tonight. They all sensed it. One could see the anticipation in the three young women's eyes. This was something new for them. Tips from high-rollers. Look sexy. Flirt a little. A little action after the game, and money left on a bedside nightstand. For the two older women, dealing cards was their way of life, and the only action they wanted to see was on those poker tables.

THIRTY-TWO

Topinka's on West Grand Boulevard was across the street from the Fisher Building. They had a great menu of aged steaks, prime rib and seafood shipped in fresh daily. Linda Murdock, the bank teller from Superior Trust Bank eyed her dessert, a freshly baked slice of cake. Across the table from her sat John Angelo. He skipped dessert and sipped on a Bailey's and cream. Linda looked up from her cake with Barbie Doll innocent eyes.

"This won't do my figure any wonders."

Angelo lit up a Chesterfield.

"Let me be the judge of that. You can't come to Topinka's and not have a slice of their famous coconut cake."

Linda smiled and bit into the cake.

They'd been dating for two months now. This Doris Day look-alike with the peaches and cream complexion who always dressed nice, but still had too many buttons down the front, was working her way into his heart. Not that he minded. Linda was smart, politically aware, good company, a great kisser. And she wasn't shy in bed, though it took the fourth date before she wanted to take her clothes off. She even left the nightstand lamp on. He was beginning to like that White Shoulders Perfume she always wore and her few freckles made her look younger than age forty. Linda got hitched right out of Dearborn's Fordson High School to a Marine who was killed on Guadalcanal in 1942. Two months later she gave birth to a girl she named Donna. Her late husband's military life insurance paid for a two- bedroom duplex in Dearborn's Springwells Park, a charming little neighborhood of small Colonial style homes laid out on lanes and cul-de-sacs.

Linda didn't smoke and Angelo liked it when she encouraged him to quit. She only drank wine in moderation, watched the nightly news with Huntley and Brinkley and never missed Sunday Mass at St. Joseph's on Rotunda Drive. Linda was that honest woman he longed for, if he could keep her. While finishing her cake she told him she was concerned about her daughter, Donna, whom Angelo had yet to meet. Donna had moved out when she turned twenty-one, got her own apartment in Palmer Park and was working serving drinks at the Roostertail on the Detroit River.

She told Angelo that Donna was somewhat of a wild child during her teen years. She didn't hear from her on a regular basis, and was afraid she might be hanging around with the wrong crowd. Angelo told her not to worry. But what did he know? He just said that to soothe a worried mother's fears. They left the restaurant, drove back to her house and made love. Afterward she cuddled close to Angelo and let him wrap his arms around her. She loved it when he moved a slow hand down her side and up the curve of her hip then to her thigh and around to her belly and pulled her even closer to him. She asked him how his day went and he told her some thing or other.

All those times he walked up to her teller window at the bank to cash his paycheck from the City of Detroit he never wore a police uniform, and she never asked what he did for the city.

On their first date, the movie *Doctor Strangelove* at the Michigan Theater, over a glass of wine at the Brass Rail, he came clean about his occupation. He was a building inspector. Somehow that lie was easier to tell than the truth. And he kept telling that lie over and over.

Angelo couldn't stomach the thought of telling this sweet widow, a woman he might be falling in love with, about the twenty year old junkie mom dead with a hypodermic needle in her arm and her naked crying one year old lying by her side he'd found early this morning in an abandoned building on Detroit's east side.

THIRTY-THREE

Rita Bain sat at one of the poker tables in the penthouse suite of the Embassy Hotel. She was all alone, sipping on a vodka and tonic while twiddling a few poker chips through her fingers. The night went smooth. There were some big winners and a couple of big losers, but Detroit's elite had a rollicking good time.

The girls made out like bandits in the way of tips, especially the redhead, Donna. Her combination of youthful charm, sexy charisma and gifted innuendo had the men ready to climb into her pants the way she worked her baby blue eyes and sassy little moves on them.

But nobody got out of line and even the dealers managed to rake in some generous tips. Rita's first big game in town was a hit. After paying off the women and the rental of the room, she managed to clear almost a grand. All of it stashed away safe and sound.

There was a soft knock on the door. Rita got up to answer. She figured it might be the maids wanting to clean up. When she opened the door, it got pushed slowly into her body, backing her up into the room and made her stumble as the man pushing her forced her into one of the big leather sofas.

Rita kept her chin up, but her knees were shaking as she watched this heavy-set man with jet black hair, a pock-marked pale face and shifty eyes circle her. He was probably in his late forties with a jaw like a park bench. He wore one of those colorful Hawaiian shirts open at the collar that exposed an ugly tuft of curly black chest hair. Over that he wore a baby-blue sport coat as wide at the shoulders as a two-car garage. His pants were tan and triple-pleated and he wore them high-rise exposing sloppy argyle socks.

There was a woman with him. She was about the same age, but slim and tall, with long straight black hair almost down to the middle of her back. She wore a black suit that fit her skinny frame like a glove, and red fishnet stockings. She had the whitest skin that Rita had ever seen and her pancake makeup was so thick you could cut it with a knife. Rita tried to choke back her fear.

"Who are you and what do you want?"

The thug slapped her hard.

Rita recoiled, held her face in her hands and tried to hold back her emotions.

The woman pulled up a chair and sat close to Rita, so close that her painted red lips were only inches from Rita's face. She reeked of cheap perfume, the kind you could pick up for seventy-five cents a bottle at Kresge's dime store.

When she spoke, it was with a thick Eastern European accent. Rita recognized the accent right off. It was Ukrainian, with the same inflection of her old man and old lady back on the farm in Saskatchewan.

"You are Rita Bain?"

Rita, antsy, tried to play it cool and looked her straight in the eye.

"Who's asking?"

The big guy lifted Rita up and held her high over his head, then slammed her body down on the sofa so hard it brought tears to her eyes and soft whimpers of fear. It hurt.

The woman moved in close again.

"We ask questions. You give answers. Like yes or no. Okay?"

Rita wiped away the tears that trickled down her cheeks.

"Okay."

"You are Rita Bain?"

"Yes."

"You ran big card game here tonight with many important people?"

"Yes."

"Where is the money?"

Rita thought on that a second. Yes or no wasn't going to cut it.

"What do you want me to say?"

Rita found herself looking at the ceiling as she got thrown again, this time across the room onto the other sofa. It hurt worse than the first. Her head caught the hard arm of the sofa. It dazed her.

The woman walked over to Rita, who lay on her stomach as she tried to clear the tears and stars out of her eyes.

The woman grabbed Rita's face and squeezed.

"Two choices. First choice, he fucks you up. No more pretty face."

The woman yanked Rita's dress all the way up over her garter belt and spanked her butt.

"Second choice, he fucks cute little bottom."

Rita sat up and yanked her skirt down, her body rigid from the adrenaline that pumped through her veins.

"Neither. I'll get you the money."

"When?"

"Look, there were important people here tonight. You know that. I wouldn't just walk out of here with a bundle of cash sticking out of my purse."

The woman grabbed another chair from one of the poker tables and pulled it up in front of Rita.

"Here is the deal I offer you. You keep your game with fancy-shmancy people. One time in week, two times, whatever you want. But we take seventy-five percent. You keep twenty-five. Yes?"

Rita had some tough times in her young life, but the last ten minutes was bad juju. She wasn't about to play games with this crew and their shake-down gig. She nodded yes.

THIRTY-FOUR

Woodward Avenue at ten a.m. on a weekday was always busy with pedestrians and traffic. People still worked downtown, even though they lived in the suburbs to the north or west. Rita Bain strolled through the lobby of Superior Trust Bank and up to a teller window. Linda Murdock was there to greet her.

"Can I help you?"

"Yes, I'd like to see Mister Harold Crosby."

"Do you have an appointment?"

"No, but he is expecting me. My name is Rita Bain."

Linda picked up her phone, talked to Mister Crosby, hung up and told Rita to have a seat in the waiting area. Mister Crosby would see her shortly.

Rita took a seat in one of the comfortable leather chairs and watched people and cars through the large picture windows. She could see just a peek of gray overcast sky between the tall buildings. It was a gloomy day and nothing appeared to be on the horizon to brighten up what happened in the last twenty-four hours.

Harold Crosby was one of the big losers at Rita's party last night at the Embassy. Hopefully he was a better bank vice-president then he was a poker player.

She met him two months ago when he hit on her at the Playboy Club. Rita started turning tricks when she got back to Detroit. She expected to find that hundred grand waiting for her in Skip Ten Eyck's safe, but that was a no go from the get go with Skip in prison and the whole operation busted up. She was lucky enough to be free and clear of that mess. She'd slept with a few guys, but never for money. Her looks commanded top price for her services and she only worked the high end of the market.

Harold Crosby was fifty years old, three years older than her father back in Saskatchewan. He was overweight and divorced, fancy free with the money and bankrolled her new high stakes poker game.

Crosby left the game the night before with all the cash and deposited it into a business bank account titled Maple Leaf Enterprises this morning. Rita was president and chief bottle washer of the whole shebang. What was in it for Crosby? Monetarily, nada, maybe he might win a few hands of poker, but with his luck and skill, cashing out big was a pipe dream. Said he didn't even want a piece of Rita's business.

What he wanted was Rita as a steady roll in the hay and the promise she wouldn't give it up for other guys. Men are so stupid, she thought, as Crosby exited his office and greeted her with a nervous smile and a voice with a slight shakiness to it.

Linda from behind her teller window watched the two of them disappear into his office and wondered what this was all about. Linda wanted to believe that this unscheduled meeting with a pretty girl young enough to be his daughter was all on the up and up.

Rita sat and listened to Crosby rant for about thirty seconds about how she should never come to see him at the office. How it might look and all that jazz before she told him to cut the shit.

"Look, I would have called but I just got the life scared out of me."

"What?"

"A woman who looked like she stepped off the Hollywood set of *The Adams Family* TV show and her goon of a boyfriend strong-armed me for part of my business."

Crosby pondered that, his eyes darting about, seeing bad news down whatever road this might be going.

"How much?"

"Seventy-five percent."

"This is a joke, right?"

It was all Rita could do to not jump across his desk and pound the crap out of him. Rattle his cage. She took a deep breath.

"Joke? The boyfriend, ugly son-of-a-bitch, with fifty pounds on you, was either going to fuck up my face or my ass."

Crosby lit a cigarette. The match shook. His deadpan face froze.

"What did you do?"

Rita couldn't believe she had to spell out all the details for this dumb as a box of rocks nerd with wire-rimmed glasses, who sat behind a big mahogany desk. His shaky hands fiddled with a brass name plate that read in all capitals: *HAROLD CROSBY VICE PRESIDENT*.

"Oh, I told him to leave my pretty face alone. I just had my makeup done at Hudson's, so have your way with my ass."

Crosby set his name plate down, embarrassed, as he tried to figure what to do with his hands.

"But they didn't hurt you."

"They threw me around enough that my body hurts like hell. I can show you the bruises."

Crosby raised an eyebrow, concerned that Rita might stand and tear off her clothes.

"I believe you. Should we call the police?"

Rita was about to hit the ceiling, but she tempered her tone a couple of decibels.

"Sure. Let's call the police. Tell them we're running an illegal high-stakes poker game at the Embassy Hotel. We have a municipal judge, couple of state legislators, attorneys from some of the biggest law firms in the whole fucking city."

"Okay. I get the message. What else did they tell you?"

"They want seven hundred today. I'm supposed to meet the Morticia look-a-like in the back row of the Madison Theater at one o'clock this afternoon."

Crosby mulled that over and tapped his fingers on the table.

"All right meet her there and give her the money."

"These people are dangerous. You want me to put my life on the line?"

Crosby got a sly look on his face, thinking he wants to let her keep the game in play.

"How many games do they want you to run?"

"Many as I want."

Crosby rolled that around in his brain, putting two and two together, thinking he could cash in on the front end. He'd collect a fee up front from each player, but wouldn't share any of it with Rita.

"Okay then, do it. I've got people on a waiting list to get in on this. You can run a couple of games a week if you want."

"That's a lot of work for twenty-five percent."

Crosby, with a hard-on suddenly for money, decided to take it up a notch and make it personal.

"You know, you were... what's the term? On the skids when I picked you up that night at the Playboy Club. You'd still be peddling your ass and making ends meet in fuck-pad hotel rooms. I saved you from that. Staked your little enterprise. Set up your private slush fund. You owe me a lot. Take a bigger rake, or I could get you a job at a teller widow out front. It pays a hundred dollars a week. How does that sound?"

Rita was feeling Crosby had the upper hand now. He'd managed to flip the switch on this and on her. This woman who could talk the legs off of a welded metal table when she had to, who nobody could beat at three card monte, needed to play her last card.

"You were born when I made love to you, you died when I left you, you lived the few months you loved me."

Crosby, dumbfounded, looked at her with anger and questions in his eyes.

"What's that supposed to mean?"

"From now on our relationship is all business with no benefits."

Crosby now looked more hurt than angry.

"You're dumping me, just like that?"

"You're loaded. Buy somebody else to love."

There was a moment of icy silence. The only sound that of traffic on Woodward Avenue.

Crosby stood up. He looked down at Rita.

"All I've done for you, and this is how you treat me. Is this how it ends?"

Rita shot him a vamp smile.

"That's the fact, Jack."

Crosby, his anger boiled up.

"How do you want that seven hundred? Twenties, fif-ties, hundreds?"

THIRTY-FIVE

John Angelo sat on the sofa in Linda Murdock's living room sipping on a cup of coffee and smoking a cigarette. The TV was running a political ad for President Johnson. It was a week before the November election and the ad was trying to scare the crap out of voters if they were thinking about pulling the lever for Goldwater.

There was a photo on the wall of the late President Kennedy. Linda was a big fan and though his assassination was almost a year ago, she would still get emotional talking about it. She wished his brother Bobby would have run, but decided she had no choice but to go all the way with LBJ.

It was Monday morning and Angelo was dressed in a dark blue suit, ready to head to work. He had a boat load of buildings to inspect today. That was the MO that he always laid on Linda, a boring job with nothing worthwhile to talk about. And she never asked. She always seemed more interested in him as a person than what he did for a living. He could hear the sound of the bathroom shower and in a few minutes she'd walk into the room in her white terrycloth robe with a matching white towel wrapped around her head and put those warm blue eyes on him, shrug her shoulders in a cute little way, sit in his lap, give him a kiss, and tell him to have a wonderful day.

God, he loved this woman, and everything about her. But his days were never wonderful and seldom boring. What he couldn't admit to himself was that the action was what kept him going, kept him sharp, gave him that edge he needed to survive in all the ugliness around him. How could he share that with a woman like Linda? Better to lie, and building inspector was a safe way out.

THIRTY-SIX

The Roostertail restaurant was hard on the Detroit River, one of the nightlife hotspots to see and be seen that mostly catered to the young single cliental. Bankers, attorneys, auto engineers, CPA's, would dress in their uniforms of black or gray Hart Schaffner & Marx suits, French-cuffed white shirts and black silk ties. They were looking for one-night stands or once-in-a-whiles.

And pretty maids all in a row would line the bar, young and lean as snakes in their skin tight cocktail dresses looking to latch onto something more permanent.

The Detroit River was famous for unlimited hydroplane boat racing. With a heavy chop on the water the big boats, powered by World War Two Rolls Royce twelve-cylinder aircraft engines, could reach speeds of one hundred and fifty miles per hour and would kick up water behind them like a rooster's tail.

The Roostertail was the best place to watch the races, if you could score a seat. But that was a summertime activity and this was November; today the place was half-empty with a more sober lunch crowd of conservatively dressed accounting clerks, secretaries, office managers, making happy chatter. The folks who kept their businesses running, who on most days brown bagged it to work were here at the Roostertail to see what the fuss was all about.

Donna Murdock was working the afternoon shift today. Her red hair was tied tight in a ponytail and she wore tight black slacks, white blouse with black bow-tie and patent leather heels. Standard cocktail waitress garb. She carried a tray of empty glasses back to her work station. That's when she noticed her mom, Linda, sitting alone at the end of the bar. Donna strolled over and said in a pleasant waitress way, "What can I get you, ma'am?"

Linda looked at her with warm eyes and a smile.

"Can we talk somewhere quiet, honey?"

Donna began in some vague way to look worried, her eyes flickered and what trace of a smile there was went away. She took a quick look around the room then focused her baby blues directly on her mother.

"Give me a couple of minutes and I'll meet you out on the veranda."

Linda Murdock stood on the Roostertail veranda and looked down at the river. It was its usual green color. She gazed out at the river. A glint of sun sparkled on ripples of water. There was a breeze and she raised her face to it, but the chill bit into her face as she pulled her coat collar up tight around her neck.

Donna came out onto the veranda sans overcoat with a solemn face. The first thing she did as she approached her mother was to light up a Viceroy with a Zippo, sucking hard to get a good draw.

"Do you have to smoke?"

"You came over here on your lunch hour just to tell me that?"

Linda's face froze, thinking she had played this all wrong. Not a good way to start this conversation.

"I'm sorry, but you know I worry about you."

"Mom, I'm twenty-one, I live on my own and I make my own decisions now."

"I know that."

There was a long pause. Linda was at a loss for words.

"Spit it out, Mom. What you're worried about is that I might end up like you."

Those words got Linda angered up a notch.

"I did the best I could. It wasn't easy raising you all alone."

"Please. Don't lay that sorry song on me again. Look at you. Miss Doris Day with your hair cut and dyed just like her, playing the forty-year old virgin. But all those different guys you'd drag home on a Saturday night. I was a little girl. You didn't think I could hear you banging them on your squeaky mattress, your dirty talk egging them on, then them tip-toeing down the stairs and out the door?"

That slammed Linda hard, but the words were true.

"I'm not drinking anymore."

"Don't blame it on booze. Not one guy you could keep around? Not one guy you'd ever let me meet? Were you looking for Mister Right, or just a Rock Hudson or James Garner look-alike?"

Even in the cold weather there was a faint glitter of sweat on Linda's forehead. Tears welled in her eyes and began to stream down her cheeks.

"Boo-hoo, that's not going to work anymore, Mom. You taught me well. But hey, I still love you."

Donna took one last drag on her cigarette, flicked it into the river, then gave her mom a curt nod.

"Don't tell me how to live my life."

Then she walked away.

Linda stood there, crying. She looked at the river, and for just an instant felt like jumping.

THIRTY-SEVEN

The first thing Rita Bain did after she left Harold Crosby's office at the bank was to walk over to Lippman's Tool Shop and Sporting Goods on the corner of Michigan Avenue and Washington Boulevard and buy a gun. A Smith & Wesson .32 caliber automatic with an eight-shot clip. The clerk, an older guy, with a creepy grin, smelled of end-of-the-day sweat and Aqua Velva.

With a condescending attitude he told her it was called a belly gun, because that's where most people carried it. He said since she had what looked to be a nice flat little belly, she could stick it in her purse. With his creepy eyes roaming over her, she almost told him where he could stick it. She bought the gun along with a box of shells. That was a couple of months ago and she never had needed to take it out of her purse.

Rita met the Morticia look-alike lady at one o'clock sharp at the Madison Theater that first time, passed her the seven hundred bucks and was told plans had changed. Next time the money would be picked up the night of the poker party. And Rita knew who'd pick it up. It left her with a hungry, hollow feeling inside.

The slob of a wrestler who body slammed her like a sack of potatoes never said a word. He walked in when the night was about half over, downed a couple of beers without paying, watched all the action, and at the end of the evening counted up all the cash, taking the seventy-five percent.

She didn't want to be alone in the room with the thug so she hired some muscle. He was sitting next to her at the bar at the Brass Rail, drinking a Miller High Life, "The Champagne of Bottled Beer", and dipping French fries in a plate of ketchup. He was black, went about six feet four and two hundred and twenty pounds, wore skin tight Levi's and a black shirt that looked like it was painted on his chiseled upper body. There was a diamond stud earring in each ear lobe.

He went by the name of EZ. Short for Edwin Zachariah. Last name Mann. EZ Mann. Now with a name like that how could he be anything but cool? He carried himself with confidence, not cocky, but with a strut in his gait. Nobody to crowd or he'd put you down hard.

EZ played two years of football at Eastern Michigan University in Ypsilanti and worked as a bouncer at the Green Cat, a nightclub out on Eight Mile. Rita called him her good friend but she didn't ride around on his back. They never fooled around. And that was okay with Rita. Besides, he was gay.

Rita was nursing the last of her double scotch and soda when she felt a hand on her shoulder and heard a soft and clear female voice.

"Laurel? Laurel Gray, is that you?"

Rita felt the blood drain from her face as she turned around and saw a skimpy dress, a fresh face and bright young eyes that flickered this way and that. It was an image from out of the past.

THIRTY-EIGHT

Skip Ten Eyck's '62 Corvette was parked in front of the gate at the Ionia Correctional Facility. The top was up and the engine running. Behind the wheel sat a young lady in her early twenties. She wore a black leather jacket over a black turtle neck sweater and tight black pegged cigarette pants that reached the top of black leather spiked heel boots.

Her red hair was pinned up in a swirl piled on top of her head. She was no stranger. Her name was Anna Capri. She was the cute little trick that was Skip's wannabe dirty movie star who got it on with the Brinks brothers for fifty bucks a pop.

The night Skip's combination grind house movie studio and reefer emporium got raided, Anna was home at Mom and Dad's in Farmington Hills, nursing a bad case of the flu. The cops never touched her and since Skip got sent up, she'd been living at home, taking tickets and dressing up as an usherette at the Redford Movie Theater part time, telling her parents that she's thinking of enrolling at Mercy College to be a nurse, and that the

Corvette stored in the garage belonged to a friend who joined the Marine Corps. Some parents will buy anything and they bought that. The whole nine yards of it.

It was a chilly November day so Anna cranked the heater up to high as she watched Skip leave the gates of the prison and walk toward her in the parking lot. He wore a cheap black suit that was too tight and too short in the sleeves and the pants showed too much of his white gym socks. Skip popped open the passenger side door and jumped in the bucket seat. Anna shot him a half-grin.

"Where the fuck did you get that outfit?"

"Salvation Army. They bring it in by the truckload. Cost me a buck and a half. It was the best I could do."

Anna leaned over and gave him a wet kiss on the lips. He held her tight for a moment before she pulled away.

"You want to run that by me again on how you're getting out so early?"

Skip peeled off his necktie, rolled down the window and tossed it on the ground.

"Three things, Sweetie-pie. Good lawyer, good behavior, and overcrowded facilities. Drive… I can't get this place in the rearview mirror fast enough."

Anna pushed the clutch to the floor, slipped the gear shift out of neutral and into first, popped the clutch and stalled the car. Skip showed some temper now as Anna flashed him a sorry look.

"Maybe you should drive."

"They yanked my license. Six months of probation, I get it back. You managed to get it here in one piece so try it again. This time let the clutch out nice and easy." Anna managed to get the 'Vette out of the parking lot, out of town, south on M-66 and east headed back to Detroit on I-96. All the while Skip badgered her about how often she started the car, checked the tire pressure, checked the antifreeze, changed the oil, blah-blah-blah. He was like a broken record stuck on the last groove.

It wasn't until she got just west of Lansing and cranked it up to sixty-five in the right lane that he finally wound down. She looked over at him, this loopy guy she stuck with not out of love, but sheer greed. There was a hundred grand out there and she wanted part of it. With a sly smile, she kept her voice calm and collect.

"Ran into Laurel Gray the other day."

That hit Skip in the face like a load of bricks.

"Laurel? Holy shit. Where?"

"Brass Rail"

"Did she say anything?"

"Said her name was Rita Bain."

"Rita Bain? You sure it was Laurel?"

"Thousand percent. She dyed her hair blonde, but I'd recognize that voice and face in an instant. It was her. She was sucking on a high-ball. Had some big colored guy with her. A pretty hunky dude with diamond earrings."

"Diamond earrings? Fuck. How much you wanna bet she bought those with my money she stole? What'd you say to her?"

"I said I'm sorry, but you reminded me of someone I once knew and walked away. Then I crossed Woodward Avenue and hung out in a hock shop near Grand Circus Park till they left the bar, followed them over to the Embassy Hotel on Washington Boulevard, and watched them get on an elevator."

There was a long pause. Too long for Skip. Anna liked to yank his chain every now and then.

"And?"

"I cornered a busboy in the bar. Nice colored kid named Benny, not more than nineteen. Asked him if guys were still taking girls upstairs for some hanky-panky. He thought I was a cop. I told him I wasn't. He asked me if I was interested in turning tricks because if I was, he could set me up with some high-end clients."

"Thought you said he was a nice kid?"

"He was. Didn't say he was honest."

Skip shot her a bitter-eyed look.

"So, Laurel's hooking at the Embassy, son-of-a-bitch."

Anna punched the Corvette up to seventy, getting the feel of the car now, driving one-handed, with the other hand on the floor shift, enjoying the moment and story she's telling.

"Let me finish. I asked Benny the busboy if he knew a girl named Rita Bain. Told him I just saw her get on the elevator with a big dude with diamond earrings. Busboy says EZ Mann.

That's the dude's name. Told me he was Rita's hired protection, her bodyguard."

Skip, his face charged with blood, was taking this all in, rubbing his hands together like a kid in a candy shop without any change in his pocket.

"Laurel's fucking big shots and then the dude rolls them for all their cash?"

Anna glanced in the rearview mirror, throttled up to eighty, waiting for Skip to react. She threw him a wink.

"Don't get ahead of me, honey-bun. If only it were that simple. Busboy Benny tells me Rita's running high-stakes poker games three nights a week in the penthouse suite on the eighteenth floor. He says he sets up the bar with close to two hundred dollars in booze. I asked him how I get in on the action. He said no dames allowed unless I want to get friendly with some of the players and if I do, he can set me up."

"What did you tell him?"

"I said set me up."

Skip fidgeted in his seat.

"Damn, so when is this poker game?"

Anna backed off the accelerator, brought the car down to forty-five, and pulled on to the service drive of a rest area. She flicked on the radio. The bad boys of British rock, The Rolling Stones, were singing *Time Is on My Side.*

"Tomorrow night, Baby Cakes, eight o'clock sharp. Check the glove box."

Skip flipped open the glove box, pulled out a small caliber revolver with pearl handles. The gat was no bigger than a Dick Tracy cap pistol and looked well used. Skip spun the barrel.

"Where the fuck did you get this antique?"

"That hock shop near Grand Circus Park while I was waiting for Laurel and her hard body boyfriend to leave the Brass Rail. Get this. The old as fuck pawnbroker says he'll give me the gun for free if I blow him in the back room."

Skip sat there rigid, eyes shining, lips parted in a sort of half-smirk.

"Tell me you paid cash."

Anna looked at him with disdainful eyes.

"What do you think?"

Skip didn't know what to think. Anna would flop for a guy at the drop of a hat.

"How much?"

"Fifteen bucks."

"Does it work?"

"He said I could bring it back if it didn't."

Skip may have gotten the shaft genetically when it came to brains, but Anna was a piece of work. She did what you told her, did it pretty well long as you told her which foot to start on and how many steps to take which way and little things like that.

Skip narrowed his eyes, gave her the Humphrey Bogart attitude.

"Now let me get this straight. We're gonna bust in on Laurel Gray's poker game at the hotel, and I pull out this buried treasure and point it at her hard guy with the big muscles and hope that he's not packing, and if he is, I fire off a couple of rounds, but if my gun's a dud, what you're telling me is we can get your fifteen bucks back?"

Anna gave him one of those come-hither smiles.

"Be right back, I have to pee."

And with that she shut the motor down, opened the car door and scooted off toward the restroom.

THIRTY-NINE

John Angelo removed his suit jacket and laid it over the work desk chair. He loosened his tie and rolled up his shirt sleeves. The heating system at headquarters was a nightmare this time of year. The heat would kick on then kick off. Too cold, then hot enough to almost fry your brain. The lights buzzed and glowed overhead as Angelo stared at the mound of paper work on his desk. Most of it leads that went nowhere.

He was still trying to track down Laurel Gray, but she seemed to have vanished without a trace. Her business partner, Skip Ten Eyck, got bounced out of prison early yesterday and that pissed Angelo off. He knew Skip would be hungry to find that missing hundred grand that was on the books. Laurel Gray beat feet with it was the conventional wisdom around the office, and Skip would be one motivated ex-con in tracking her down.

Angelo checked his watch that read ten forty-five, lit up a Chesterfield, picked up his empty coffee mug and headed down the hall for his third cup of the morning.

As he passed Homicide Division he looked in and noticed a woman sitting alone at a detective's desk. Her hands were in her lap and her head was down. He recognized her immediately. How could he not. It was his girl, Linda Murdock. Angelo opened the door, entered and walked slowly toward Linda.

"Linda?"

Linda gave him a quiet up from under look.

"John?"

There were questions in her eyes that were wet from tears as mascara streaked down her cheeks. And then suddenly it hit Angelo like a brick up the side of the head. He stood there motionless for what seemed to be an eternity. He saw Linda look at the police badge pinned to his belt. Her eyes then moved up to the holster and .45 automatic that hung from his left shoulder. His building inspector charade just crashed and burned. Linda wanted to say something but the words were not there.

"Angelo. Is it too hot for you over in Vice?"

It was Captain O'Dowd, Angelo's former boss when he worked Homicide, standing outside his office door.

Angelo tried to make eye contact with Linda one more time, but now her eyes ignored him as she buried her face in her hands. Angelo walked over to O'Dowd.

"Can we talk, in private?"

O'Dowd walked into his office and Angelo followed, closing the door behind him.

O'Dowd took a seat behind his desk.

"Are you going to tell me how you know that woman out there?"

Angelo walked to O'Dowd's desk.

"Why is she here? What the fuck is going on?"

O'Dowd lit up a fifty-cent cigar and blew out a plume of smoke that hung in the air.

"I knew it. Let me guess. Your new girlfriend."

Angelo got hot under the collar as the sweat rolled down his face.

"You didn't answer my question."

"Okay. Her daughter Donna Murdoch got strangled last night at the girl's apartment in Palmer Park near the Detroit Golf Club."

That hit Angelo hard. So hard it put him in a chair.

"Did she find her?"

O'Dowd eased up, seeing the grief on Angelo's face.

"She hadn't heard from her daughter in a couple of days. Drove over there this morning before work to check on her."

Angelo blew out a breath he'd been holding in.

"Details?"

"The girl was naked face down on the bed, a pair of nylons wrapped around her neck. The medical examiner's checking for signs of sexual assault, but the preliminaries don't look good."

Angelo leaned forward in his chair. A dead-blank look on his face as he stared at the floor. O'Dowd stubbed out his cigar and walked over to Angelo and put a hand on his shoulder.

"Drive her home, John. I'll have someone get her car back to her house. Take the rest of the day off. Be there for her. I'll clear it with Vice."

Angelo stood, ready to leave.

"Thanks."

Angelo headed for the office door.

"One thing, John. I was just wondering, since you're a cop, why she didn't call you first."

FORTY

The drive back to Linda's place in Dearborn wasn't that far, but the silence in the car made it seem like the longest journey of Angelo's life. He didn't know what to say. Angelo came with his own atmosphere, his own weather. You could look at him and not really know who he was. He hid his inner demons behind good looks and easy charisma. And all that was worthless right now.

They pulled into the drive and Angelo shut the motor off. Linda sat there a moment and then spoke for the first time. She didn't look at him.

"There must have been a reason you lied to me all these months but it's not something I want to hear right now."

The early morning sun beamed through the windshield making this somber moment too bright.

"Do you want me to come in with you?"

Linda hung her right hand over the door handle.

"No. I called a friend earlier. She's coming over to stay with me."

She opened the car door, put one foot on the ground and for the first time since they left police headquarters, she finally made eye contact with Angelo. It was all there, written on her face. Grief, sadness, betrayal, but not anger. Linda got out of the car, looked back in at Angelo, her voice hardened.

"It's going to take time. Or… maybe there isn't enough time. But until you own your own soul, John, you can't be part of mine."

Linda's words stung Angelo hard, hitting him clean and quick like the blade of a knife going deep.

Angelo watched her enter the house. He put the dashboard lighter to a cigarette and inhaled, sitting there a few minutes thinking what a dumb-ass he was. Here was the best woman he'd ever known, someone he loved dearly who returned that love unconditionally with honesty and devotion.

He started the car, backed out of the drive and made his way back to the office. Heading east on the Edsel Ford freeway the bumper-to-bumper traffic frayed his nerves. His mind buzzed with words and images. A jumble of running thoughts. He couldn't focus on anything longer than a few seconds. Maybe he didn't deserve Linda. Maybe all he was good for were broken women. Maybe he should call Velma Turnbull and drive over to her place in Windsor and let her fuck his brains out.

He couldn't even remember pulling into the underground parking garage at Headquarters. But there he sat in his numbered spot with the motor running. When he shut the motor down, he sat there, motionless, closed his eyes and dozed off.

There was a loud rap on the driver side window of Angelo's car. It startled him out of a half-sleep. He rolled the window down and looked at a uniformed cop.

"Captain O'Dowd wants to see you over at Superior Trust Bank on Woodward, there's been a shooting."

Angelo checked his watch. He must have slept a good hour.

"I'm Vice, not Homicide. What the hell does he want to see me for?"

"Don't know, but he sure sounded like it was important."

FORTY-ONE

John Angelo and Captain O'Dowd stood by the dead body of Superior Trust Bank vice-president Harold Crosby who was slumped over his desk. A .38 caliber Smith & Wesson revolver was clutched in his right hand. Blood covered the top of the desk and the entire left side of his temple was blown out. O'Dowd was chomping on an un-lit cigar.

"The bullet went clean through, exited the left side, and lodged in the molding over there by the window."

Angelo took a closer look at the body.

"Looks like a suicide. Why am I here?"

O'Dowd handed Angelo a letter.

"Found this in the top drawer of his desk. It's a little weird, but it sounds like a confession."

Angelo read the letter out loud.

"I was born when you kissed me, I died when you left, I lived the short time you loved me."

Angelo handed the letter back to O'Dowd.

"Confession? Confession to what? Sounds like a piss-pour attempt at bad poetry. Who's it to? There's no name, no nothing."

Angelo was trying to see the whole picture.

"Yeah, it's weird. Maybe a note to some dame he was fooling around with?"

O'Dowd flipped through Crosby's Rolodex on the corner of the desk.

"This might be a stretch. Maybe it's right out of the catalogue, maybe not. There are all kinds of names, addresses and phone numbers in this Rolodex. Some of them I recognize, businessmen, lawyers, doctors, politicians. People you'd normally expect to see in a banker's Rolodex."

O'Dowd stopped on one of the cards, pulled it out.

"Here's a name I never expected to see. A female, her address… Palmer Park Apartments."

O'Dowd handed the Rolodex card to Angelo.

"He just wrote down her first name, Donna… your lady friend's daughter."

Angelo stared at the card for a long moment. Shocked. A cold light in his eyes.

"It's not a stretch. I never met the girl, but Linda was worried about her, said she was kind of a free spirit. Thought she might be involved with the wrong kind of people."

"Other than Crosby being more than twice her age you wouldn't think a bank vice-president the wrong kind of people."

Angelo handed the Rolodex card back to O'Dowd.

"If you can piece this all together, can you make it stick?"

"There were finger prints all over the girl's apartment. If they match Crosby's we've got our killer. Older man, younger woman, she gets tired of him, wants to move on, so she pushes him out. He gets angry, strangles her with her own nylons, comes to work the next day full of remorse, writes a sappy love poem, then puts a bullet through his brain. Would make a great movie, but I think Hollywood's already done a couple dozen of them."

"When can you get all the lab work wrapped up?"

"Tomorrow morning at the latest, I'll push them on it. You want to tell the mom about her daughter's relationship with Crosby, or you want the Department to handle it?"

Angelo thought hard on that, realizing what that meant.

"When you lock it down that Crosby was the killer, send over a couple of women. The social worker that works Juvenile and Sandra from Robbery. Linda's had enough hard-edge men in her face lately giving her bad news.

FORTY-TWO

Anna Capri strutted into the bar at the Embassy Hotel looking like a one hundred dollar a night hooker, wearing a tight black dress that fit like a wetsuit, and stiletto heels. She'd dyed her hair copper blonde earlier that morning with it falling away from her bedroom eyes like Veronica Lake in the movie *This Gun for Hire*. The one where Alan Ladd can't take his sassy eyes off her. A spattering of people sat at booths and round tables drinking and laughing, and no one at the bar other than a bartender with a face full of nothing and eyes that had as much expression as a door knob. He perked up when Anna took a seat.

"Welcome to the Embassy, Miss. What can I get you?"

Anna tilted her head to one side, brushed her hair away from her face.

"I'll have a vodka martini, very dry with two olives. Is Benny the busboy around?"

The bartender flashed her a sly look.

"Benny called in sick, but I can fix you up."

"Fix me up?"

The bartender's eyes were puffy and his hair cropped close to his skull like the old prizefighter that he was in his younger days. The slow way he spoke the result of too many punches to the head.

"Honey, of all the slumming angels that stroll in here, you are one cute little number worth playing around with. How much you get for a night? Or do you work by the hour?"

Anna didn't know whether to flash him a dreamy look and take that as a compliment or scrunch her face up and look pissed off. She decided to go with dreamy.

"A little birdie told me some big money high rollers are playing poker tonight upstairs in one of your fancy rooms. Any way I can tap that action?"

The bartender shot her a sneer.

"A tall torcher, a blonde with a bottom bigger than that barstool you're sitting on and a beautiful smile, but on the wrong kind of face, brought a house full of law in here couple of months ago. You one of those undercover chicks?"

Anna knew she had to stay one jump ahead of this dick-head in the bartender costume.

"Nope."

The bartender was steady as a rock.

"Now I value your business, but not enough to cut my own throat and bleed in your lap."

Anna pulled a pack of Pall Malls from her purse and lit one up, blowing smoke across the bar into his face.

"You ever see a cop as hot looking as me?"

That appeared to be good enough for the bartender.

"I can give you a room on the same floor. That'll cost thirty. You don't need to check in at the front desk. I got keys. When the poker game's over there'll be a knock on your door. That'll be a John, or Jack, or Jim, whatever the hell his name is. You didn't tell me how much you charge."

Anna wanted to play it cool, but suddenly her lips seemed to have forgotten how to work and she hesitated, not having thought about money before she dolled herself up.

The bartender was getting impatient.

"Speak your piece, Princess Barbie."

The lug was starting to grate on Anna, so she threw out a number.

"Three hundred dollars."

"Whoa, hot girls like you come in here a dime a dozen and wanna-be party girls are a nickel a gross, but I never heard a number like that. You got a guy walks behind you?"

"A what?"

"You know, your hard boy, your pimp."

"Yeah, what about him?"

"Well here's the way it goes down. You wait in the room and I send the john up after he forks over the three hundred. I keep twenty percent. After he's shot his wad or whatever, he better not come stumbling in here with a frown on his face asking for a refund."

Anna knew she wasn't the sharpest tool in the box but she knew how to satisfy a man and the look in her eye was like strange sins.

"The only thing on his face will be a bigger than this barstool grin."

The bartender leaned in, rested his elbows against the bar, and looked her straight in the eye.

"You are one foxy little dame."

Anna took another drag on her Pall Mall.

"I have a question."

"Yeah, what's that? But I don't budge on the twenty percent."

Anna leaned her elbows on the bar, almost nose to nose with the bartender, her voice deep, rich, down around the ankles.

"Where's my martini?"

FORTY-THREE

Room 1821 at the Embassy Hotel was about fifty feet down the hall from the penthouse suite. The furniture was old and worn and there were stains on the carpet that looked like either blood or booze, but probably both. The bed was a double and sagged at one corner.

Anna Capri sat in an overstuffed chair by the window twisting a strand of hair between her fingers. She stopped fooling with her hair long enough to take a swig from half a bottle of vodka she managed to chisel off the bartender for letting him sneak a peek down her dress. She sat there quiet as a church parishioner waiting for communion.

The toilet flushed in the bathroom and out walked Skip Ten Eyck. Anna looked up at him with a tinge of disgust.

"You never wash your hands."

Skip shrugged and stuck his hands in his pockets.

"What're we gonna do when a dude shows up?"

Skip arrived in the room ten minutes ago. Anna called him at the pay phone over at the Brass Rail and gave him the room number. He was jumpy, but Anna's been able to calm her nerves with several hits of the vodka.

"I've been thinking about it."

There was a soft knock on the door. Anna took one last swig of vodka and stood up.

"Get in the closet and don't make a peep."

Skip ducked into the closet and closed the door. Anna sashayed over to the door and with a lustful smile on her face, opened it. Standing there were three young men, clean cut, maybe eighteen, dressed in suits and ties. One of the young men tried his best to play it cool.

"Wow, look at you. Isn't this going to be fun?"

That lustful look on Anna's face was replaced by surprise and a shade of panic in her eyes.

He gently pushed his way into the room followed by the other two. Anna stepped out of the way.

"Where are the other two girls?"

Anna had to think fast, not something that was up her alley. These guys were too young, probably virgins. Maybe never been past first base with a girl. She flashed them a sly smile.

"How much did you pay the bartender and what did he tell you?"

One of the other boys piped up.

"He said there were three hot babes in room 1821, one hundred dollars each."

Anna rolled that around in her head for a couple of seconds, hiding her anger.

"Well boys, he lied, so I guess I'm the only entertainment for the night."

The three boys looked at each other with grins on their faces like cats about ready to eat the canary. One of the boys took a step toward Anna.

"What's the deal? How are we going work this?"

Anna tilted her head forward at an angle, let her hair cover her left eye, her voice sexy, right out of the movies.

"Well, first we all get naked."

And in what seemed like a blink of an eye, Anna kicked off her shoes, peeled out of her dress, unhooked her bra, dropped her panties and garter belt to the floor, sat in the chair and pulled off her nylons, then stood there bare assed naked in front of them. The boys were startled like it was the first time they'd ever seen a grown woman in her birthday suit. Anna stunned them with a smile and wink.

"Okay, boys, don't be bashful, now it's your turn."

The boys looked at each other. Not sure about this. Embarrassed.

Anna reclined in the big chair and crossed her legs.

"Go ahead, don't be shy. I'll just watch."

The boys started removing their clothes, but not in any hurry, taking off this and that, looking for places to hang coats and shirts, ties, underwear, and avoiding looking at each other. Anna was laughing inside.

"Just let it all drop on the floor. No need to be prim and proper."

When they were all naked, they stood there, choir boy faces, hands in front of their privates, acting like the whole world was watching. The one boy wasn't so cool anymore.

"Now what?"

Anna seductively walked into the bathroom.

"We're going take a shower. Get all squeaky clean."

"A shower? You mean one at a time?"

"No. All four of us together, real cozy like. Rub-a-dub-dub."

The boys looked at each other. That sexual bravado they walked in with gone, replaced by a sudden bout of prurient hesitation. They were like little boys now. Rich spoiled amateurs. One of them whined.

"Do we have to?"

Anna grabbed their arms, slapped them on their bare bottoms, and pulled them into the bathroom.

"Didn't your mommas scrub you up when you were little babies?"

Anna turned on the shower.

"Go ahead, get in. I've got to tinkle first."

Anna plopped herself on the toilet as the boys all stepped into the tub.

She yanked the skeleton key out from the door, jumped up, closed the door behind her and locked it.

"Skip."

Skip came out of the closet as fast as Anna started getting her clothes back on.

"Get their clothes, Skip."

"What?"

"Their clothes… pick up their clothes."

"Why?"

"Do I have to spell it out for you? The window, stupid, throw their clothes out the window."

Skip let that sink in a couple of seconds, then scooped up the clothes, threw open the sash, and tossed them down onto Washington Boulevard.

FORTY-FOUR

Rita Bain sat at one of the poker tables in the penthouse suite at the Embassy Hotel playing tricks with a deck of cards. No one was at the other two poker tables and the only other person in the room was EZ Mann who stood behind the fully stocked bar looking for something to drink.

"No Miller High Life? All you got is Stroh's? Thought you told the busboy I liked Miller."

Rita palmed the cards with one hand flipping them one at a time suit side up on the table.

"Won't kill you to drink a Stroh's."

EZ cracked open a miniature bottle of Wild Turkey, poured it into a glass, dropped in a fistful of ice.

"You know, something's not working here like it's supposed to. It's almost eleven. Game starting late or you getting stood up?"

Rita messed with the cards, a tinge of anger in her eyes, thinking Crosby's paying her back for kicking him out of her bed. It was just like him. He couldn't let it go. Getting all flirty with the girls on poker nights, even the older dealers. Playing kissy-face and lovey-dovey with Donna the bartender in front of her and the players. Later bragging to Rita about getting his ashes hauled at Donna's place over in Palmer Park. What a great lay she was. The fucking creep.

EZ strolled over to the TV and flicked on channel four, the eleven o'clock news, the anchorman reading off the teleprompter.

"Police are still investigating the murder of Donna Murdock at her apartment in Palmer Park last night. Police are keeping mum on any motive, but say they are investigating several leads. In another story, police are ruling the death of Superior Bank Trust Vice President Harold Crosby a suicide, taking his life in his office this morning. Up next, tomorrow's forecast."

EZ switched off the TV and shot a quick look at Rita. The slow, numbing beat of the anchorman's words hit her hard. EZ downed the last of his drink.

"What do you think?"

Rita tossed the cards, got up from the table, grabbed her purse.

"I think we should've watched the six o'clock news. Let's get the hell out of here."

The penthouse door burst open and coming into the room like gangbusters were Skip and Anna all rough and blustery. Skip's eyes tossed with fury, the cheap Smith & Wesson that Anna bought at the hock shop shaking in his hand, his face popping sweat.

"Where's the party, boys and girls?"

Skip shoved Rita onto one of the sofas as EZ took a step forward. Click. Skip cocked the hammer back.

"Hey, brother, don't like the sound of that."

Skip pointed the gun at EZ's forehead.

"Well, it's gonna get a lot louder if I pull the trigger. Now kiss the wall, shit bird, I got no beef with you. We're all aces, okay?"

EZ put his hands over his head and faced the wall. Anna, tipsy from the cheap vodka she'd been belting back, sat at one of the tables, kept her mouth shut, and gave Rita a half-assed attempt at a stink eye. Skip turned the gun on Rita.

"Laurel Gray, Rita Bain. Got any other handles up your sleeve?"

Rita rolled her eyes.

"Skip, you are one eager beaver, putting all your heart and soul into this, aren't you? Even brought Anna along for backup. Look at her. She's not half-in-the-bag, she's eighty proof. I know what you want, and I don't have it."

"Don't try to flim-flam me. There was a hundred-grand in that safe right next to your desk. Cops said it was gone. I didn't take it, sweet cakes over there didn't take it, and that leaves you."

Rita eased back into the sofa, getting as comfortable as she could, showing no fear, or hiding it pretty good.

"You don't scare me, Skip. You have the stones to use that pop gun? I told you, I don't have your hundred-grand. If I did, would I be hanging around on the eighteenth floor of this flop house of a hotel, or would I be sipping a rum and Coke at a villa in the Bahamas?"

Anna was feeling the booze, screwy drunk now and figured it was her turn to throw in her two cents worth.

"Don't let her dummy up on you like that, Skip. Put a little heat on her."

Rita laughed.

"Speaking of heat, how's the movie business treating you, Anna? Got any break-out hits coming our way?"

"You're just jealous because you couldn't do what I can do in front of a camera. Why I'm pretty enough to be on TV. Isn't that right, Skip?"

Skip's clammed up, thinking the conversation's getting away from him.

Rita said, "Yeah, Anna, you're smart enough and pretty enough to be on TV… pointing at game show prizes."

Anna, with voodoo eyes, started to come out of her chair. Skip gave her a scolding glance.

"Sit down and zip it."

Anna scrunched her face up in a scowl, sat and lit up a Pall Mall. Skip put his focus back on Rita.

"You were the last one to open that safe when you paid the Brinks brothers. I didn't touch it. When the cops raided the place, the money was gone. They think I stashed it away somewhere. Tell me where the money is or I'll put a bullet in your buddy here."

"Hold on there, ace. If she told you she doesn't have the money, she doesn't have the money."

Rita was having a brain tease about what Skip just said about the Brinks brothers and the safe and the money gone. She got up from the sofa and took a step toward Skip.

"Okay, I took some money, but not one-hundred grand."

The door to the room popped open and in stepped the big thug in his Hawaiian shirt coming to get his usual seventy-five percent from Rita's poker night. Skip spun around and pointed the gun at him. The thug's voice was like a sledgehammer busting concrete.

"Where's the money?"

Anna jumped up, got right in his face, all cigarette and arched eyebrows and go-to-hell expression.

"Who the hell are you Mister shirt full of pink and green flowers with your cream-colored fancy pants? Did some faggot dress you? You're not getting any of our money."

It was the vodka talking, and not much up there in the way of common sense. The thug slapped the cigarette from her lips, put one hand around Anna's throat and the other hand in her crotch, lifted her high in the air and heaved her half way across the room into the radiator. Her neck hit the sharp edge of the metal snapping it in a loud crack. The life drained from Anna's eyes.

Skip put the gun on the thug.

"You dick."

And pulled the trigger. Click. It misfired. The thug came at Skip hard and fast. Skip pulled the trigger again. The gun went off loud. The shot ripped a hole in one of the pink flowers on the shirt as it penetrated the thug's barrel chest. Before Skip could get off another round, the thug put him in a bear hug and pushed him toward the window. Ka-Boom. Glass exploded as the two of them crashed through the glass and tumbled down to Washington Boulevard, Skip screaming all the way.

Freefalling eighteen floors didn't take but a couple of seconds. Rita and EZ heard them hit something, but they didn't bother to see what. They ran from the room, down the hall and beat feet down the stairs three steps at a time to the lobby and out the back door just as they heard prowl car sirens race up Washington Boulevard. They got in EZ's 1954 Ford Victoria and gunned it down a side street headed for the Lodge Freeway.

FORTY-FIVE

The roof of a new Buick Riviera parked at the curb on Washington Boulevard was crushed down to the door handles. The crash-landed bodies of Skip Ten Eyck and Mister pink and green flowers were smack-faced embraced. Stuck together like glue. Blood trickled down to the street. Reporters took notes while photographers looked for better angles. Plainclothes cops packed Winchester pumps as the entire street was packed with patrol cars, red lights still spinning. Uniformed officers kept the looky-loos at bay. It was a scene right out of a cops and robbers TV show.

Upstairs on the eighteenth floor of the Embassy Hotel in the penthouse suite John Angelo sat at one of the poker tables playing solitaire. EMTs carried the body of Anna Capri away on a stretcher, bumping into police Captain O'Dowd as he sauntered into the room chewing on an un-lit cigar.

"How'd you get on this so quick, Angelo?"

"I'm righteous Vice, we go where the action is."

O'Dowd got a laugh from that.

"It's a three-ring circus down there. The Riviera is registered to one Victor Schenk, the guy on top in the Hawaiian shirt. Know him?"

Angelo was still busy with his game of solitaire.

"Yeah, used to be a pro wrestler. Lower tier. High school gyms, Knights of Columbus Halls. Never made it to the big show. No Dick the Bruiser, but liked to throw people out of the ring. That was his specialty. Called himself the Big Hawaiian. He was the muscle for a half-assed gang of Ukrainians. Dope, slots, illegal vending machines."

O'Dowd lit his cigar.

"Well, the Riviera was no more than a week old. No way to break in a new car. Skip Ten Eyck, guy who got sandwiched, I know he's been on your radar. Tell me what you got."

Angelo ended the game, folded up the cards, got up and walked to the broken window and looked down onto Washington Boulevard.

"Skip had aspirations but mush for brains. I've been watch dogging him ever since he got sent up. He was after a hundred grand and a girl named Laurel Gray who went missing with it."

O'Dowd kept puffing on his cigar.

"So why did he end up here at poker night in Detroit?"

"I squeezed the hotel bartender and he sang like a canary. Seems a girl named Rita Bain's been running games here for a couple of months. Skip gets sprung yesterday, shows up here with

Anna Capri, his porn princess, looking for his money, and they both end up crashing into heavy metal objects. Rita Bain and Laurel Gray are the same girl. There are prints all over this room, mine included. They'll find Laurel Gray's prints here, guaranteed."

O'Dowd walked over to the window and stood next to Angelo.

"Are you saying she threw a few hundred pounds of pro-wrestler and an ex-con out here all by herself?"

"Bartender said she had some protection with her, guy named EZ Mann."

"EZ Mann? That's got to be made up."

"Don't know about that, but I know he's a bouncer at the Green Cat over on Eight Mile. But I'd bet a month's pay Victor Schenk, The Big Hawaiian, with his arms wrapped around Skipper, rode him down onto his new set of wheels without being pushed or thrown."

O'Dowd turned that over and tried to put it together.

"All those names in Crosby's Rolodex, how much you want to bet they liked the action here?"

"Bartender told me he's seen a few City Councilmen and some well-dressed businessmen on some nights, but nobody showed up tonight. I figure Crosby ran the operation, brought in the players and Laurel Gray, Rita Bain whoever she is, ran the games."

"How does Vice want to handle this?"

"I don't want to fight City Hall or half the law firms in Detroit. Let's keep the names in the Rolodex out of the papers. It isn't worth the hassle."

There was a long pause as they looked down at Washington Boulevard and scoped the ruckus. O'Dowd turned to Angelo.

"What's with all those clothes scattered all over the street? I walked by a VW flying a pair of Jockey shorts from the antenna."

Angelo grinned, turned away from the window, leaned against the wall and lit up the last Chesterfield in the pack.

"What's so funny?"

Angelo took a drag, inhaled deep, with that grin getting wider, flashing his good-guy look.

"Few doors down the hall, room 1821, there are three boys, high school seniors. They all decided to go skinny-dipping in the bathtub. If you walk down there, it's a wild-ass tale if you want to hear it."

FORTY-SIX

Rita Bain sat behind the wheel of EZ Mann's Ford Vicky parked at the curb in front of a cracker box of a house in the Salinas area of Detroit, south of Ford's River Rouge Plant. The house hadn't seen a paint brush in decades and was almost down to bare wood. It was a ragged-ass, neglected neighborhood, and the street Rita was parked on was still dirt from horse and buggy days, and not on any city commissioner's wish list to get paved.

Rita left EZ at the Green Cat on Eight Mile about forty-five minutes ago and told him she needed to borrow his car for a last-minute errand. EZ was slack-jawed when she told him that, and asked her to go around on that again. She leveled with him the best she could. Her ass was tainted. He had a clean record. The cops would believe what he'd say about what went down at the hotel. Just tell them that he was muscle, if it came to that, protection for her, Rita Bain who hired him a couple of months ago. Don't know anything about her. And that was the honest to God truth so there was nothing to lie about.

Rita gave EZ a hundred bucks and told him she'd leave the car in the parking lot at Ernie's Liquor Store on John R downtown. And that maybe there might be something extra for him in the trunk. She'd leave the keys under the gas tank flap. She told him this wasn't bullshit. He was better off going it alone now. She'd be a weight around his neck. EZ was smart enough to buy what she was selling. He told her to have a nice life, wherever that might be.

Rita looked in her purse, got out of the car and walked up the brick sidewalk to the old house. She could hear the sounds of the Rouge Plant not a quarter mile away. The constant roar of the coke ovens and blast furnaces hurt her ears and the smell of sulfur, and steel being made burned when she breathed. When she stepped onto the front porch, she could see the black coal dust soot from the plant that had settled everywhere, and she could taste the grit in her mouth. She wondered how any human or living thing could exist here. It was the bottom of nowhere. Maybe it would smell better inside the house. She sucked in a breath, got her courage up and knocked on the door.

When Cliff Brinks opened the door, he stared down the barrel of Rita's .32 Smith & Wesson. The gun she bought at Lippman's Tool Shop & Sporting Goods store. The gun she loaded that day and stuck in her purse. The gun that stayed there until tonight, now clutched comfortably in her right hand as her pulse banged in her ears. She pushed Cliff into the living room.

"Long time no see, Cliff. Or are you Roger? Never could tell you two apart."

Cliff's smug drunk grin filled his face.

"Why Laurel Gray, that's because you never seen the two of us buck naked in the flesh."

He got a big laugh out of that. Laurel, not so much.

"Where's your brother?"

"Roger done joined the Army."

"Army? You're lying."

"No, God's truth. Roger got busted breaking into washing machines at the Fresh & Clean Laundromat over on Fort Street. Judge told him two years or the Army. Roger took a burst of three wearing Army green rather than two in prison stripes. They put him in Military Police. Ain't that a joke? Now he's overseas in someplace called Saigon guarding a three-star general."

"Well how patriotic of him. You know why I'm here?"

Cliff shuffled his feet, took a step back, trained his eyes to the dirty wood floor.

"Yeah, but there ain't no money."

"Don't bullshit me. You and your brother took that safe out of my office, didn't you?"

"Yup, you're right about that. Used a dolly and rolled it right down the stairs, out the back door and into the back of my F-150."

"There was a hundred thousand dollars in that safe. What did you do with all that money? Obviously, you didn't spend it on home improvement."

Rita looked around the living room, the place was a dump, the walls plastered with pinups galore, mostly centerfolds ripped from girlie magazines and a couple of dated gas station calendars, girls with big lungs hiking their skirts up.

Rita kicked a couple of smutty magazines and stepped on a copy of *Confidential* with Elizabeth Taylor and Richard Burton on the cover. Empty bottles of PBR were tossed helter-skelter. The furniture was dark and soiled and from another time, with a couple of aluminum lawn chairs, the webbing starting to fray and an old black and white TV tuned to an episode of *Gilligan's Island*.

Cliff, with his hands up, beamed a smile.

"Why don't you put that gun away? Can I get you a beer? You're making me miss my favorite TV show. That Mary Ann is one hot little piece."

"Shut up, you pervert."

Cliff brought one of his raised hands down onto Rita's gun hand, but she was too quick for him. She kicked him away and put a hard foot into his crotch. He doubled up with pain sucking wind. He whimpered.

"Shit. Why'd you go and do that for?"

"It'll sting a while, but I'm sure your plumbing will work just fine. Now show me that safe."

Hunched over and holding his balls with both hands, Cliff led Rita through a kitchen full of cockroaches homesteading on pots, pans and plates coated with moldy food that looked as if they hadn't been washed in years. He led her through a fenced in backyard filled with busted and dented cigarette and candy vending machines. On the ground in pieces were several gumball machines. Rita took a disgusted look at them.

"Bubble gum machines? You've got to be kidding."

Cliff was still feeling the pain from Rita's foot.

"You can get twenty bucks in pennies from one that's full up."

Cliff led Rita into an old double garage packed with junk over to a safe that had the door open and what looked to be the residue of burned paper money. He turned to her.

"There ya go. You said a hundred grand? Well that's what's left of it."

Rita couldn't believe her eyes.

"Don't try to scam me you son-of-a-bitch. Where's the money?"

"Ain't no scam. Roger took a cutting torch to it and ended up welding the combination dial to the door. Then we tried blowing the hinges off with a stick of dynamite. That almost brought the fuzz down on us. It blew the door open but all that money caught fire. It was hotter than one of those blast furnaces up at mother Rouge. Sorry."

Rita couldn't believe what she was seeing or hearing. Dumb is dumb, but this was a whole new reality. She took one last look at the safe and then a cold x-ray eye at Cliff, lowered the gun and stepped closer to him. So close she could feel and smell his hot tobacco-beer breath. And then she brought the gun hand up quick and sucker punched Cliff in the nose with the barrel.

It pushed him onto the garage floor, as his surprised dopey face filled with blood.

Rita turned and walked away, out of the garage, through all the clutter in the back yard, and heard Cliff laughing and yelling.

"Hey there Laurel, I know you don't like being called a dope-peddling whore, but you ever wanna make a movie with me, I know where I can get a camera."

The last thing Laurel did before she left was stomp a cockroach on the kitchen floor. It was deliberate. And it felt good.

FORTY-SEVEN

John Angelo pulled out of his parking spot at police headquarters and aimed his Chevy toward Jefferson Avenue. It was four in the morning and he'd spent the last two hours grilling EZ Mann and coming up with nothing. Angelo and EZ went back a couple of years and EZ was always appreciative that Angelo never came down hard on any of the gay bars in Detroit. The way Angelo figured it there was enough illegal stuff going down all over the city so why bother chicks with other chicks and dicks with other dicks. Long as they did what they did out of public view.

EZ told Angelo everything he knew about the whole gambling operation, which was not much. Rita Bain ran the whole show. She never told him who the players were. All he knew was they had money to burn and talked like they had educations. The only thing EZ didn't tell Angelo was that his Ford sitting in the parking lot next to that liquor store over on John R was left there by Rita. It wouldn't have made any difference because later when EZ popped open the trunk, the only thing in there was the spare tire.

Angelo knew that you could never bat a thousand working Vice. You'd be lucky to bat three hundred. He didn't want to figure the percentages on the last couple of years. Too many people ended up dead and that gnawed on him. But it was Laurel Gray working as Rita Bain and the missing money that made him feel he wasn't even in the game anymore.

Angelo parked his car on the street outside his apartment, checked his mail, took a shower and climbed into bed thinking he could catch a couple of winks. He tossed and turned. He'd had nothing but bum sleep three nights running. What kept him awake were thoughts of Linda Murdock. It hadn't even been a couple of days and he missed her already. He wished he could go back in time. Back before the war and not volunteered to work combat military police. Not joined the police force. Not switched over to Vice. Not seen all the brutality he'd seen.

He wished that he could have been a building inspector and that when he met Linda and told her what he did it wouldn't have been a lie and they'd be married now. It was a dream, but he wasn't sleeping. It was the reality now, and the thought of not ever seeing her again was the nightmare.

FORTY-EIGHT

A Greyhound bus pulled to a stop in the middle of nowhere. The destination flip sign read Vancouver, but this wasn't Vancouver. It was the desolate prairie of Saskatchewan. The wind was blowing and the moonlight was so sharp that the black shadows of the bus could have been cut with a knife. The bus door opened and out stepped Yelyzaveta Petrenko. She wore a trench coat buttoned up under the chin against the cold night. Her purse was slung over her shoulder and she carried a single suitcase that she set on the ground as the bus pulled away and disappeared into the night. Yely, that's what her kindergarten teacher pinned on her, telling her Yelysaveta was too hard to pronounce, pulled the collar of her coat up around her ears to shield her face from the cold wind.

It was a wind that never stopped blowing. A wind that drove some of the first settlers mad back in the 1800's, especially the women cooped up in their drafty sod huts twenty-four hours a day. Yely's parents settled here after leaving Ukraine in 1930 and established a wheat farm about forty miles west of Moose

Jaw. Yely was an only child and from the time she was five years old helped with the chores around the farm.

As Yely stood there staring off into the nothingness her stomach began to ache. She hadn't eaten in over twenty-four hours and was down to her last five dollars, barely having enough money for bus fare out of Sault Ste. Marie. She wished she could have given EZ Mann more than a hundred bucks. Getting her hands on the five G's in her business account, Maple Leaf Enterprises at Superior Trust Bank back in Detroit was a pipe dream.

But that was all behind her now and what she saw coming from the west was a car with one headlight out. God, after all these years was that her mother's 1950 Ford sedan that kept burning out the driver side headlight? The same car Yely drove that night to the Junior hockey game in Moose Jaw right after she got her license at age fifteen. The same car that cute hockey player from Regina hitched a ride with her back to his motel out on the highway. But they never got that far. He made her pull over in a park near the river and raped her in the back seat. Then he made her drop him off at the motel. She never told anyone and never wanted to drive or ride in that car again.

As the car came closer, she hoped it wasn't the old Ford. That it would be a Chevy or a Plymouth. It stopped, and it was her mother's Ford and it was now on the opposite side of the road. Yely, anxious, walked to the driver side window as it rolled down and she recognized her father behind the wheel. He looked older than his fifty some years. His weathered face was hardened and cracked from the wind and sun. She looked in at her dad and the empty passenger seat.

"Mom didn't want to come?"

Her father took a moment to respond, his face tightened. He struggled to get the words out.

"Mother died last year."

Those words hit Yely hard. Her face went blank. She wanted to cry, but the tears weren't there. She tried to say something but what do you say after you've been gone all these years and come home to find your mother dead?

She looked in the window to the back seat. A little girl, maybe five or six years old was curled up sound asleep wrapped in one of those Hudson Bay blankets. It was her daughter. It had to be. She had the same dark black hair and round eastern European face. Yely didn't even know her name. She looked at her father whose stoic face stared straight ahead, his eyes following the lone beam of headlight as it lit the two-lane blacktop.

"Dad, okay if I ride in the back?"

"You can ride wherever you want."

Yely opened the rear door and climbed into the backseat. Quiet. Move slowly. Try not to wake the child. She eased the car door closed. The little girl rustled some, but didn't wake. Yely put her right arm over her daughter, comforting her as the old Ford drove away.

FORTY-NINE

The Springwells Park neighborhood of Dearborn was breathtaking. A sight to behold in the springtime. Flowers bloomed out in pinks, yellows, reds, blues and greens. The large magnolia tree in Linda Murdock's front yard was thick with white flowers. If you stood under it looking up you couldn't see the sky. It was late May, 1965, and all of southeast Michigan was having an early heat wave with temperatures in the 80's and stifling humidity.

John Angelo stood on a ladder in Linda Murdock's duplex living room installing a curtain rod over the front window. It took a couple of months, but Linda eventually let him back into her life. Didn't make him jump through any hoops. Didn't make him sleep in the downstairs bedroom. All she did was tell him that if he ever lied to her again, he'd have to pack up all his stuff and scram, this time for good. That was the hard edge of it so Angelo was doing his best to keep on her best side, helping out around the house, sticking an AC unit in the bedroom window upstairs, going to Mass with her Sunday morning at St. Joe's and trying to stay awake during the sermon.

It was a Monday and Linda's day off since she usually worked the Saturday morning shift at the bank. And the only day of the week she could watch Bill Kennedy's movie show on channel nine. Kennedy was a former Hollywood 'B' actor who hosted a daily afternoon show, Monday through Friday. He showed old movies from the '30's and '40's and during commercial breaks blabbed about his days in Hollywood, dropping names of stars he worked with and hung with. Linda loved old movies and Kennedy's rat-tat-tat chatter.

There were two TV tables set up in front of the sofa and Linda came in from the kitchen with lunch for both of them on two plates. She set them on the tables, clicked on the TV and headed back to the kitchen.

"I'm having a beer, you want one?"

"Yeah."

Angelo watched her walk out of the living room. She wore Bermuda shorts, a tight-fitting t-shirt that read *Henry Ford Community College* and nothing on her feet. As he watched her head into the kitchen, he thought about what their love making used to be like. Her blonde hair against his face. That soft white body. Her show-class breasts.

Linda struggled with the death of her daughter and he missed that gleam in her calm eyes. When she asked him if he wanted a beer, he probably should have said no. The ginger ale in the fridge would wash those ham sandwiches down okay. Linda wasn't a heavy drinker, but lately was hitting the beer and wine too hard. He saw it in her tummy and slight bulge under her chin. She saw it also, but said a drink every now and then relaxed her. Said it took her mind off things, made her doze off easier. She had trouble sleeping, and some nights he could hear her crying in the bathroom downstairs.

He knew she was popping pills, bennies, to keep her awake during the day, but he couldn't find where she hid them and he didn't want to push her on it. The sex wasn't as frequent as before but she was more aggressive. He sensed anger in her when they made love, but not at him but someone else, maybe at herself?

They ate the sandwiches, drank their beer and listened to Bill Kennedy introduce today's flick, *In A Lonely Place* staring Humphrey Bogart and Gloria Grahame. Bogie played a washed-up Hollywood screenwriter named Dixson Steele who had a hot temper, a real prick, and Gloria was the doll-faced woman who lived in the apartment across the courtyard who tried to tame him.

When Angelo heard her character's name for the first time he almost choked on his sandwich. Laurel Gray.

He didn't say anything, ate his sandwich and asked Linda to get him another beer. She did, and one for herself. Near the end of the movie with Dixson and Laurel driving in a convertible, Dixson ran a line by Laurel. A line he wanted to use in a new script he was writing. It was the same line that Harold Crosby wrote in his suicide note before he blew his brains out. Angelo's jaw almost locked-up when he heard those words. The crap about getting born when she kissed him, dying when she left, and living a little when she loved him.

Angelo wanted to say something, maybe scream out loud. But he didn't. What good would it do to lay this on Linda? He couldn't soft-peddle it. So he sat there in stoic silence, watched the rest of the movie, then listened to Bill Kennedy babble about how five packs a day of Lucky Strikes killed Bogart and how Gloria's promising movie stardom led to an Oscar for the flick *Oklahoma,* but lately she'd been showing up in bit parts on TV.

Linda pushed her TV table away, got up and clicked off the television, turned to Angelo, and noticed his sour face.

"What's the matter, you didn't like the movie?"

Angelo took the last swig of his beer, lit up a Chesterfield, and eased back into the sofa.

"Movie was great, what's got me half-ass restless, I'm seeing only half the picture."

Linda sensed his irritation.

"What do you mean?"

"The chick's name in the movie, Laurel Gray, same name of a broad that disappeared on me. A case I crapped out on. Dead-ended on. The department shit-canned the whole fucking investigation."

Linda was not about to second guess what was going on.

"John, you've been retired for a month now. You have to learn to let it all go. You could start by losing the seedy cop lingo."

Angelo sat there and puffed on his cigarette a moment.

"This Laurel Gray's been bugging me for months, then it turns out she's using the name Rita Bain."

Linda tried not to react when she heard that familiar name.

Can I get you another beer? I'm having one."

"No, make it ginger ale."

Linda walked into the kitchen, took a deep breath and let it out. She whispered, "Holy fuck, Rita Bain?"

Linda always considered herself a good Catholic. She'd get after Angelo for swearing, but rationalized as long as she never swore out loud then she wouldn't have to confess it and say all those Hail Mary's.

Should she tell John about a young girl named Rita Bain who walked into the bank a few months ago and asked to see Harold Crosby, and spent a good half-hour with him in his office? If she did, one thing would lead to another and she'd confess to John how Harold Crosby, that awful man, the man who fucked and murdered her daughter, spent many nights in her bed upstairs. And she'd have to lie about not liking it.

Angelo kicked his shoes off and reclined on the sofa. He thought about the case that got away, but Linda was right, he had to let it go. His mind turned to the movie. No happy ending. Bogart and Grahame didn't hook up at the end. That's life, he thought.

He closed his eyes and wondered about his own relationship. Was this going to end the same way? Maybe it would work out. Maybe Linda was the right one, maybe not. There was always Velma Turnbull across the river in Windsor. He didn't want to spend any time thinking about that.

Linda came back into the living room with a Stroh's and a ginger ale. She stood in front of Angelo. He looked up at her sweet face with the fine spray of freckles. This fragile beauty had a gleam in her eyes that he hadn't seen in months. She leaned in close, handed him his ginger ale, then sat in his lap.

"Hey, lover boy, how about we go out dancing tonight?"